He was d[...]
beyond e[...]

"I've had enough!" Angrily, Charley threw her machete to the ground.

"Backing out, are you," Braden sneered. "It was you who wanted to be treated as an equal."

Charley replied furiously. "No, I'm not backing out. I actually think I'm doing all right, and if you were man enough, you'd admit it, too. What is it with you that you're always so hard on me? Is it frustration because I won't give myself to you? If that's all you can think about, then I pity you!"

His eyes grew cold and his mouth hardened. "It's obviously what's on *your* mind...."

Charley couldn't deny it. Not only were the impossible hardships pushing her over the edge—but Braden's unsettling nearness was as well....

Margaret Mayo began writing quite by chance when the engineering company she worked for wasn't very busy and she found herself with time on her hands. Today, with more than thirty novels to her credit, she admits that writing governs her life to a large extent. When she and her husband holiday—Cornwall is their favorite spot—Margaret always has a notebook and camera on hand and is constantly looking for fresh ideas. She lives in the countryside near Stafford, England.

Books by Margaret Mayo

HARLEQUIN ROMANCE

2385—BURNING DESIRE
2439—A TASTE OF PARADISE
2474—DIVIDED LOYALTIES
2557—DANGEROUS JOURNEY
2602—RETURN A STRANGER
2795—IMPULSIVE CHALLENGE
2805—AT DAGGERS DRAWN
2937—FEELINGS
2955—UNEXPECTED INHERITANCE

HARLEQUIN PRESENTS

963—PASSIONAGE VENGEANCE
1045—SAVAGE AFFAIR
1108—A PAINFUL LOVING
1187—PRISONER OF THE MIND

Bittersweet Pursuit

Margaret Mayo

Harlequin Books

TORONTO • NEW YORK • LONDON
AMSTERDAM • PARIS • SYDNEY • HAMBURG
STOCKHOLM • ATHENS • TOKYO • MILAN

Original hardcover edition published in 1988
by Mills & Boon Limited

ISBN 0-373-03003-7

Harlequin Romance first edition September 1989

CHAPTER ONE

'I MUST go, Mom. It's the only way we'll ever find out what's happened to Daddy. I can't sit around and do nothing. I wish I'd gone with him.' *And then they might have both disappeared!* It was a frightening thought. Charley pushed it firmly to the back of her mind.

Isobel Blake's face crumpled with pain, and it was obvious she was thinking the same thing. But they had tried every other means. No one, not even the Peruvian authorities, who had shown so much interest in Spencer Blake's trip, could tell them what had happened to him. He had disappeared without trace.

'But what if I lose you as well?' Isobel's eyes were tearful as she looked at her daughter. 'What would I do? I've never liked you or your father going off on these trips. They're insane, Charley.'

'But we enjoy them, you know we do.' Charley's blue eyes pleaded with her mother. 'I blame myself for not accompanying him this time. I have to go. You can't talk me out of it.'

'I suppose if Alan went with you . . .?' ventured the older woman doubtfully.

Charley nodded. Her battle was won. 'I wouldn't dream of going alone.'

Charley was the Blakes' only child. Spencer had dearly wanted a son, and his disappointment was made even more acute when Isobel was told after

Charley's difficult birth that she could have no more children. He had bought his daughter guns and cars instead of dolls and prams. He had played football with her and taken her climbing and pot-holing. Her black hair was cropped short and she wore jeans and shorts and never skirts. By the time she was thirteen she was a thorough tomboy, and by the time she was sixteen she had developed her father's passionate interest in archaeology, and in particular the lost cities of the Incas.

She was absolutely fascinated by the subject, reading every book she could on it. Her father had not needed much persuasion to take her with him on his frequent explorations in Bolivia and Peru, Brazil and Colombia, and all the rest of the known Inca empire. She had loved every minute. She loved the jungle; it wasn't full of wild animals but tranquil and beautiful. She loved the excitement, the exhilaration of discovering something new.

Only on this last trip had she disagreed with her father. Usually she was the first to say they would go. But when Rupert Billings had come up with a story about a previously undiscovered Inca city in Peru she was very sceptical, especially when the archaeologist who had supposedly discovered it had never returned. The tale had been told by an Indian who claimed to have gone most of the way with him. Privately, Charley thought the Indian was out to make money by selling his story.

'Dad, you always said that the lost city of the Incas was in Bolivia.'

'But I could be wrong.'

'And you're going to chase out there on nothing more than—hear say? Rupert Billings is a romancer, you should know that.'

'But there might be some truth in it,' insisted her father. 'I have to find out. It's an area we haven't previously explored.'

'And it's an area you'll explore on your own,' she said crossly. She did not like Rupert Billings, convinced he spun her father tales just for the sheer hell of it.

Her father's eyes widened. 'You mean you won't come with me?'

'No.' Charley shook her head. 'It's a wild-goose chase, I'm sure of it. Don't ask me why, just feminine intuition. Please don't go.'

But her father had been adamant and they had had their first real argument. Now he had disappeared like the other archaeologist, and Charley wished with all her heart that she had been more insistent that he did not go. Or at the very least that she had gone with him.

It puzzled her. Had he really found the lost city of the Incas? El Dorado, as the Brazilians called it. Paititi as it was called in the western half of South America. City of Gold as some other people called it.

Had he found this exalted place and lost all idea of time as he explored it and filmed and recorded it? Or had something terrible happened to him? Had he met a group of hostile Indians and been killed? Had he become too ill to make it back home? Charley recalled the months he had once spent in the Hospital of Tropical Medicine in London. They had only just got home in time on that occasion.

'Alan's sick,' Charley told her mother flatly as she put down the telephone. 'He can't come.'

Isobel Blake's face paled. 'You're not thinking of going alone?'

'I don't know anyone else I can trust,' she shrugged. Alan Ross had accompanied them on several expeditions. He was as experienced as her father, and knew the way Spencer's mind worked. He was the perfect choice for a partner.

'There is one other man,' said her mother, 'if you're still determined to go.'

'Of course I'm determined. For goodness' sake, don't you care what's happened to Daddy?'

'I'm worried out of my mind,' replied Isobel Blake, 'you know I am, but I don't want you endangering your life as well.'

'I'll be all right,' said Charley dismissively. 'Who've you got in mind?'

'Braden Quest.'

'Braden Quest? We can't ask him.' Charley's blue eyes were wide with astonishment.

'I don't see why not, if we make it worth his while.'

'No.' Charley shook her head. 'He wouldn't.' Braden Quest was a legend in his own lifetime, one of the world's leading anthropologists, with special interest in the Inca culture. Intrepid, brilliantly clever, a mind as sharp as a razor. He had written books on the subject, made films, given frequent lectures, and Charley knew all about him, though she had never actually met him.

Her father had met him once, and he had gone on for weeks afterwards about what a talented and fearless man he was. If anyone could find her father it was he, but it was unlikely he would bother himself. If her father was fool enough to get himself killed, or lost, or taken prisoner, then he had only himself to blame and should never have gone in the first place. That was what he would say, she felt sure. He would have no time for people who could not take care of themselves.

'Then we'll never know whether your father's dead or alive,' said Isobel Blake sadly.

'I thought you didn't want me to go,' frowned Charley.

'I don't. But if you were with Braden Quest I'd have no worries.' Ready tears sprang to the older woman's eyes. 'I can't sleep at night, Charley. I lie awake imagining all sorts of horrors. I'll never rest until I find out what's happened.'

'Nor me,' agreed Charley. 'If you know where he lives, I'll write to him at once.'

Three days later Braden Quest turned up on their doorstep. Charley answered his knock and immediately recognised him. He was taller then she had imagined. Well over six feet. Broad and powerful. Deeply tanned with grey eyes that missed nothing and a nose that looked as though it had once been broken. His mouth was full and wide, and there was a jagged scar down one cheek. His fair hair was cropped short and he wore black suede trousers and a black knitted silk shirt that strained across his muscular chest.

The strength of him was almost tangible, as too was his air of authority. Success sat on his shoulders like a mantle. 'My name is Braden Quest,' he said. 'I'd like a word with Charles Blake.' His voice was deep and intensely sensual and Charley could not help being affected by it. This was some man.

She smiled warmly. 'I am Charles Blake. Do come in. I never expected you to——'

He cut in on her peremptorily. '*You*—are Charles Blake?' There was disbelief in his eyes.

'That's right,' she assured him. 'I apologise for

my name, but my father wanted a son.'

He muttered something under his breath which Charley could not quite catch, and then said more audibly, 'In which case I'm wasting my time. Good day, *Miss* Blake.' And turning smartly on his heel he retreated down the path.

For a second Charley could only stand and stare. *He was going.* Because she wasn't a man he was going! He wasn't going to help them. She sprang into action. 'Wait! Mr Quest, please wait. I can assure you that I'm as good as any man. I——'

She tailed off as he turned around and impaled her with his eyes. His head was at an angle, and due to a trick of the light his eyes glittered like silver. She was powerless and suddenly speechless.

'You think you're as good as a man, eh?' He looked her insolently up and down, taking note of her length of leg—she had played tennis earlier and still wore her shorts—and the pert thrust of her tiny breasts through the thin blouse. She had just finished brushing her dark hair, which she had let grow in recent years. It now fell below her shoulders and was thick and heavy, framing her face attractively, though she was unaware of this. Charley was not very tall and knew she looked fragile, but beneath she was as strong and tough as most men.

'Tell me, Miss Blake,' he went on, 'what manly attributes do you give yourself, apart from your name?'

Taking exception to the contempt in his tone, Charley tossed her head haughtily. 'I have accompanied my father on many of his expeditions and I think I can safely say that my stamina equalled his.'

'You can fight your way through virgin jungle, climb

mountains, cross dangerous rivers?'

'Yes,' she snapped.

'You can trap and cook your own food?'

'Yes.' Well, almost, her father had always done the hunting.

'What would you do if a snake bit you?'

Charley eyed him levelly. 'It's very rare you get bitten by a snake in the jungles of South America. Normally they head away from you. It's only if you do something stupid that they attack, and then they don't generally inject poison. But in any case I would apply a light tourniquet and I would always carry anti-snake-bite serum in my medical kit.'

She had thought to impress him by her knowledge, but he still looked disbelieving, as though he doubted that she had the physical strength and experience to tackle the Peruvian jungle.

At that moment her mother appeared behind her. 'Who is it, Charley?' And then her eyes alighted on their visitor. 'Oh, Mr Quest. I had no idea. Do come in. How good of you to call. I'm sick with worry about my husband.'

Charley had inherited her fragile appearance from her mother, and now Braden Quest fell beneath Isobel Blake's wide imploring blue eyes. In her forties, she was still a beautiful woman who turned many a man's head, though she had never had eyes for anyone except her husband.

There was an air of helplessness about her, and at this moment a haunting sadness, and Braden Quest followed them into the house.

'I was under the impression that Charles Blake was your son,' he said once they were seated.

Charley thought it sounded like an accusation, and her temper began to rise.

'A mistake many people make,' admitted Isobel with a rueful smile, and then on a sudden note of alarm, 'It doesn't make any difference does it? You will still help? That is why you're here.'

'I came to talk it over. To find out exactly what happened.'

'I told you in my letter,' announced Charley tersely. She was not sure that she liked Braden Quest, after all. He looked like every woman's dream, but it stopped there. His attitude was condescending to say the least. Going out to Peru with him would not be a pleasant experience.

'You explained that your father had apparently disappeared.'

'*Apparently?*' she questioned angrily. 'It's been over three months since he left. He would have got a message to us some way if he was extending his trip. He *has* disappeared. Even the Peruvian authorities cannot help us.'

'Or won't,' said Braden Quest sharply.

Isobel looked distressed. 'Please, let's not argue over it. Mr Quest, I really am desperate. Charley wants to go to see if she can find him, but I won't let her go alone. Will you go with her? I know of no one else I can ask. Just name your price. Nothing is too much to ensure the safe return of my husband.'

'He might be dead,' said Braden Quest brutally.

Isobel closed her eyes and Charley glared at him. Had the man no compassion?

'I'm well aware of that,' said her mother at length. 'But at least I'll know. You have no idea what it's like——'

'Do you know the exact route that he took?' he cut in sharply.

Charley saw the relief on her mother's face.

'Rupert Billings can tell you,' answered Isobel quickly.

Braden frowned. 'Who is he?'

'The man who encouraged my husband to make this trip.'

'How much does he know about the Incas?'

'Nothing,' spat Charley. 'He just *thinks* he knows. And I'm quite convinced that he sent my father to his death. Someone else went before him and he hasn't returned either.'

Braden drew in a harsh breath, and his eyes narrowed as he looked at the two women. 'Give me Rupert Billings' address.'

While her mother searched, Charley sat in uncomfortable silence. It was unlike her to be ill at ease in a man's company, but this was no ordinary man.

At this moment he was lost in thought and she was able to observe him unnoticed. She wondered how he had got that scar on his cheek. Had he been clawed by a wild animal, or was it a knife wound? Had he encountered a tribe of hostile Indians? And that broken nose—had it happened at the same time? Had he other scars on his body? Her eyes travelled over the bulging muscles in his forearms to the hard, flat stomach and the suede trousers that were moulded to powerful thighs. He looked formidable.

When she returned her gaze to his face Braden was watching her and Charley felt the blood rush to her cheeks.

'Well?' he said.

'Well what?' she demanded. He had caught her at a disadvantage. She imagined that this man always had a slight edge over other people, and this was not the way she liked things. Charley regarded herself as equal to any man. There was not much she couldn't do. She had had a tough upbringing, and it was a unique experience to find herself face to face with a man who made her feel inferior.

'What's your opinion of me?' He sat back in his seat, his long legs stretched out before him, his eyes half closed, his thumbs hooked into the pockets of his trousers.

'I already know all about you,' she said.

'That wasn't what I asked.'

She regarded him steadily. 'As a matter of fact you're nothing like I imagined.'

Thick brows rose. 'No?'

'No. In looks you are. I've seen you on television. But your cynicism never came across. Don't you like women, Mr Quest?'

Her question surprised him, and he sat up and leaned towards her, a sudden gleam in his silver-grey eyes. 'Oh, yes, I like women. What man doesn't? But you don't look as though you'd last two minutes in the jungle.' His gaze swept over her yet again, not missing one inch of her anatomy, and Charley wished she'd had time to change. She felt naked.

'Appearances can be deceptive,' she said, and there was an answering light of battle in her cornflower-blue eyes.

'I think it might be best if I went looking for your father alone,' he announced calmly.

Charley's head jerked. 'No way.'

'I have no intention of being held back.' His tone was firm now.

'You won't be.' Brave words when he was so much more physical than she. His long legs would cover the ground twice as quickly, and those sinewy arms would wield a machete through the bushes and undergrowth like a hot knife through butter. Charley could not deny that she found it hard going hacking her way through virgin jungle. This man would be impatient with her slowness, whereas her father had merely helped and encouraged.

'You sound very sure of yourself,' he derided, his mouth twisted scornfully.

'I'm no novice. I've been going with my father ever since I was sixteen.'

'You don't look much older now.'

She tossed her head. 'I'm twenty-four.'

He eyed her for several long seconds without speaking, and Charley began to grow angry. He was obviously weighing her up and finding her wanting. She wished she had never asked him to help.

'Why didn't you go with your father on this occasion?'

Charley grimaced. 'Because I didn't believe Rupert Billings. He's always coming up with some tale or another.'

'Is he an explorer himself?' Charley shook her head. 'Then where does he get his stories from?'

'Friends of friends,' she shrugged. 'Who knows?'

'Your father obviously believed him.'

'It's been his lifelong ambition to find the lost city of the Incas.'

Braden's lip curled. 'In my opinion there's no such place.'

'You think my father's a fool?' bridled Charley, eyes flashing.

'I said no such thing. He's not the only one with that ambition.'

'Here we are.' Isobel Blake returned to the room. 'Sorry I've been so long.' Charley was grateful for her intervention.

Braden took the slip of paper and put it into his pocket.

'Can I offer you a cup of tea?' asked the older woman, looking from her daughter's flushed face to the steady grey gaze of their guest.

'Thank you, that would be nice,' he said.

Charley groaned inwardly. She had hoped he would go. 'I'll make it,' she said, springing to her feet. 'You sit down, Mother, and talk to Mr Quest. I'm sure you have plenty of questions you want to ask him.'

But Isobel Blake shook her head. 'I think it's you two who should be doing the talking. You have plans to make, and once Mr Quest knows what's involved he must tell us how much he's going to charge.'

'There will be no charge,' said Braden Quest at once. 'Two men have disappeared, that's sufficient to arouse my interest. The only reservation I have, Mrs Blake, is about taking your daughter. I'd prefer to go alone, or at least to choose my own partner.'

'I can understand that,' said Isobel. 'How do you feel, Charley, about——'

'Nothing will stop me from going,' she spat at once, incensed by the way he was trying to get her mother on his side. 'I don't need Mr Quest. I'm perfectly capable of——'

'Charles,' Isobel put her hand on her daughter's arm, 'don't distress yourself. Mr Quest has a perfectly valid point. He'll be able to travel much more quickly without you.'

'And what do you know about it?' snapped Charley. 'Has my father ever complained that I've been a hindrance?' It was the first time she had ever spoken so rudely to her mother, and she blamed Braden Quest.

'Well, no,' admitted her mother. 'He always says you do very well, but——'.

'There you are, then,' cut in Charley sharply. 'If Mr Quest won't allow me to go with him, then he needn't bother to go at all. I'll find someone else who won't object to a female partner.'

Braden Quest pushed himself to his feet and headed towards the door. 'I don't think I'll bother with that tea Mrs Blake. It's obvious we've both been wasting each other's time. Goodbye. I wish you success.'

Charley stared from Blake to her mother, and Isobel's mouth fell open. 'Mr Quest, *no*,' said the older woman quickly. 'I mean, I'm sorry, but this means so much to me and Charley. And I know of no one else who I would entrust her to. Alan Ross was going with her, but unfortunately he's been taken ill with appendicitis and——'

'Alan Ross?' he frowned. 'I know Alan. He was prepared to go with your daughter?'

Isobel nodded. 'He's accompanied both Charley and her father on several occasions. He thinks she's marvellous. He's forever singing her praises. Says he's never met another girl like her.'

Braden Quest took another long, slow look at Charley and she felt an unexpected surge of awareness. Apart from everything else he was a disturbingly sensual man, though he did not use his sensuality. In fact, he did not even seem aware of it. But none of her feelings showed in her eyes. She looked at him coolly and suffered his appraisal in silence.

'Perhaps,' he said, 'I'm misjudging you, Miss Blake. Maybe I should have that cup of tea and get to know you better before I make my final decision.'

Isobel smiled her relief. 'I'll put the kettle on.' And before Charley could move she left the room.

Braden settled back into his chair and waved his hand airily for Charley to do likewise—as though he owned the place, she thought indignantly. When she was seated he said, 'Tell me about some of the trips you've made with your father.'

Charley began hesitantly at first, and then as she warmed to her subject she became more enthusiastic, relating incidents and discoveries in a quick, amusing manner that drew an occasional smile to his lips.

'I think,' he said, when Isobel finally returned with the tray of tea, 'that perhaps your daughter's appearance belies her capabilities—if what she tells me is true.'

'Of course it's true,' said Charley quickly and angrily. Hell, did he think she was making it up?

'And I've decided that I'll take her with me,' he went on as though she had not interrupted. 'Even though I do still have some reservations.'

'Oh, thank you, Mr Quest,' breathed Isobel Blake gratefully. 'I'm sure you won't regret it.'

There was such blind faith on her face that it nauseated Charley and she certainly felt no such gratitude. It was clear he still thought she would be a burden and she wished she could tell him to his face what she thought of him. But she must put her father first. Without Braden Quest she did not stand much chance of finding him, even though she would have had no hesitation in going alone had he continued to refuse.

'Everyone calls me Braden,' he said to her mother.

'Very well, Braden,' she smiled, 'and my name's Isobel. I do appreciate you giving up your time like this to search for Spencer. I'll be forever in your debt.'

'Think nothing of it, Isobel. If your husband's still alive, I'll find him. Actually, you were lucky to get hold of me. I spend most of my time in Peru these days. I'm researching another book, so it makes sense to live there.'

Charley was no longer listening; her mind had run on to the search that lay ahead, to the hours and days and weeks that she would spend in the sole company of this man. Could she endure it? Would he treat her as an equal? Or would he talk down to her all the time? It would be up to her to show him how tough and resilient she really was.

At length he stood up and shook Mrs Blake's hand. 'I shall be ready to leave in two or three days.' And to Charley, 'I think we should get to know one another. I hate going on expeditions with a stranger. I'll book a table for dinner tomorrow night. I'll pick you up at eight.'

Charley's eyes widened. Just like that. He wasn't asking her, he was telling her! 'I'm sorry,' she said coldly, 'I already have a date.'

Her mother frowned, knowing full well that her daughter was lying.

'Then cancel it,' he said crisply.

Charley opened her mouth to protest, but closed it again as she caught her mother's eye. She nodded almost imperceptibly.

'Good,' he said, turning at once to leave the room, her mother following him out to the front door. Charley fumed.

'Don't you like Braden?' were Isobel Blake's first words when she came back.

'No,' said Charley at once. 'He's too full of his own importance.'

'He's a very clever man.'

Charley's eyes widened. 'Even so, he doesn't have to put me down.'

'It's understandable when he doesn't know you,' said her mother reasonably.

'He didn't even take my word that I was experienced. It wasn't until you mentioned Alan.'

Isobel nodded. 'It's as well I did.'

'I'm not so sure,' said Charley. 'I don't think we're going to hit it off. I wish we hadn't asked him. I'm certain we could have found someone else to go with me.'

'He's the best.'

Charley grimaced. 'He's not the best when it comes to giving a girl confidence. I always thought I was pretty good, now I find myself doubting whether I'll be able to keep up.'

'Nonsense,' said her mother strongly. 'He's sure to make allowances.'

Was he? She wouldn't put it past him to make things as difficult for her as he could. But she didn't say this to her mother. 'No one else has ever needed to,' she said instead.

'Then you're worrying for nothing,' replied Isobel.

'We'll see,' said Charley. 'And why did he have to ask me out?' This was something else she could not understand.

'He has his reasons.'

Charley sniffed. 'Like trying to convince me he'd be better off alone.'

'I don't think so, love,' said her mother calmly. 'It's perfectly obvious he needs to get to know you.'

'We'll have plenty of time for that in Peru.'

But whatever Charley said it was obvious her mother was on Braden Quest's side, convinced that if anyone could find Spencer it was he.

The next evening Charley was ready and waiting when Braden pulled up outside the house. It had taken her a long time to decide what to wear, and in the end she opted for an amethyst tunic top with close-fitting matching trousers. It was quite dressy, yet she felt comfortable in trousers; she always did. Her make-up she kept to a minimum; a hint of mauve eyeshadow and a touch of rose-pink lipstick. She left her heavy silken hair loose.

She opened the front door and he looked at her long and hard, but made no comment. 'Would you like to come in?' she offered, struck anew by his raw masculinity, by the height and breadth of him, feeling a sudden unexpected quickening of her senses. This was something she had not expected.

He wore black trousers and shirt and an ivory jacket. He smelled faintly of musk and his blond hair was freshly shampooed, looking as though he'd had it trimmed again, even though it was already quite short. He had a well-shaped head and thick brows that were slightly darker than his hair, and he was easily the most masculine man she had ever met.

'I don't think so,' he said. 'Our table's booked and I don't want to be late.'

Her mother was out anyway, so Charley was relieved, closing the door behind her and following him to his car. It was a long, ferocious red monster that roared into life the second he turned the key, just the sort of car she expected him to have.

He took her to a tiny restaurant in the town centre. It had not been open long, but was already earning itself quite a reputation. It was furnished in Victorian style with a black-lead fireplace and pretty flowered curtains and tablecloths, with arrangements of dried flowers on the tables and bowls of pot-pourri on the windowsills.

Charley had not been there before, and looked about her with interest, and Braden had to ask her twice what she would like to drink. 'I'm sorry,' she said. 'A gin and tonic, please.'

They sat at a table in the bar and sipped their drinks
and studied the menu, and Charley was conscious of
Braden's leg close to hers.

She found herself concentrating on him instead of
the menu, and when he asked her whether she was
ready to order she gave a tiny start of surprise.

'You weren't even looking,' he accused. 'You were
miles away. What were you thinking?'

Charley would not have told him had he offered
her a million pounds. 'About my father,' she lied.

'Talking about Spencer is not the purpose of this
evening,' he said. 'The escalope of veal looks good. I
suggest you try that, and for starters the spinach
soufflé.' He beckoned to the hovering waitress and
gave their order, and Charley wondered why she had
sat back and let him take over.

It continued like this for the rest of the evening. He
led the questions, invariably getting his answers. He
was a skilful conversationalist.

She told him that at the moment they ran their own
sports shop. 'It's my father's really, but we all chip
in. That's why we're able to go on our various
expeditions. My mother never minds being left in
charge, and since Dad disappeared it's given her
something to occupy her mind.'

'But she'll be completely alone when you leave her.
Will she cope with that?'

Charley eyed him suspiciously. 'I hope you're not
suggesting again that I don't go, because it's not on.
The idea was for someone to come with *me*. You seem
to be taking over, Mr Quest.'

'*Mr* Quest? You called me Braden a few minutes
ago.'

'Did I?' she questioned tartly. 'It must have been a

slip of the tongue.'

'I think it's time we left.'

Charley gladly finished her coffee and pushed back her chair. Braden paid the bill and took her arm as they went down the steps to the car park. She felt an unwanted awareness course through her, and she would have snatched free except that she did not want to give him the pleasure of knowing that he disturbed her.

Then in his car he leaned across the seat and kissed her. Charley responded by slapping his face. He grinned. 'I'm glad you did that. If you'd kissed me back I wouldn't have taken you with me. The last thing I want on this trip is a woman who's after sex.'

'With you?' she demanded coldly. 'Never! That's one thing you can get very clear in your mind.'

'Then we should make a good pair,' he said, 'because the feeling's mutual.'

Charley wondered why she felt disappointed.

CHAPTER TWO

THE next day Charley found it difficult to push
Braden Quest out of her mind. She did not want to
think about him, she tried her hardest not to, but
always her thoughts centred on this man. His kiss
had shocked her and slapping him had been
instinctive, yet she could not ignore his overt
sexuality. The sudden rush of feelings when he
touched her set him apart from other men.

She had never felt this way before. At the age of
twenty-four she had had plenty of boyfriends, but no
lovers. She had never had time for meaningful
relationships. Most men she met were either of the
same kind as her father, loving the danger and excitement of exploring alien territory, and sex was the
furthest thought from their minds, or else they could
not understand her and kept a respectful distance.

This man was different. But the fact that he
doubted her, that he thought her incapable of coping
with the arduous journey, would no doubt dampen
any emotional feelings she was stupid enough to
entertain. It would take all her energy and single-
mindedness to prove to him that she was no helpless
female, that she was as capable as he when it came to
forging their way through the Peruvian jungle.

When he telephoned a couple of days later, she did
not recognise his voice. It sounded deeper and more
sensual.

'Miss Blake?' He obviously had no such trouble.

'Yes, who is that?'

'Braden Quest.'

She immediately felt a fool for asking, and her tone was sharp when she said, 'Do you want my mother?'

'Why would I want your mother, when I can speak to you?'

Charley thought she heard innuendo in his voice. But surely not? Braden Quest had no interest in her, none at all, he had made that perfectly clear. She waited to hear why he had rung.

'My plans are complete. We're booked on the nine forty-five from Heathrow tomorrow. I trust your paperwork is in order. Passport, smallpox certificate? You've been vaccinated for yellow fever, typhoid, cholera?' He rattled the questions off as though he were an official.

His brusque manner needled Charley. 'It's a bit late to ask me that, isn't it? Of course they're in order.'

'It's the little things that get overlooked.'

'I've not much else to think about,' she snapped. 'Whether I like it or not, I seem to have put myself in your hands.' There was a slight pause, and Charley could almost imagine the way his mind was working. 'Is that all?' she asked impatiently.

'I'll pick you up at half-past six. Make sure you're ready.'

'I will be.'

'And' Charley, don't bring too much luggage.'

She wanted to tell him that she knew all about travelling light in the jungle, but she held her tongue. 'No, Mr Quest.'

She heard his swift intake of breath and smiled to herself as she put down the receiver.

'Was that Braden?' asked her mother.

Charley nodded. 'We're leaving tomorrow morning.'

'Thank goodness!' breathed Isobel. 'I don't think I can bear the uncertainty much longer. I've kept hoping we'd hear from your father so that it wouldn't be necessary for you to go, but——'

'Me, too,' admitted Charley. 'But I'm sure we'll find him. Maybe he has found the lost city, after all, and he's so excited that he's lost all sense of time. You know what he's like. Won't he be surprised when I turn up?'

But Isobel Blake knew her daughter was only trying to cheer her up and her smile was wan. 'I won't sleep a wink until you come back.'

Charley herself hardly slept that night, and when Braden Quest arrived she was ready. She wore cotton trousers and a flowered blouse that she intended offering to the Indians they met on their travels in exchange for information. It was amazing how much these people coveted pretty clothes. Her hair still hung loose about her shoulders, but once they reached Peru Charley intended braiding it on top of her head.

Braden wore a lightweight suit, and she guessed he would pick up his travelling clothes in Peru. Charley was excited and wished it was a normal expedition instead of a search for her missing father.

He looked down at her haversack sitting waiting in the hall, and the thin nylon bag beside it. They looked nothing for the several weeks they could be away, but there was no indication on his face that he approved of her sparse baggage.

Instead he touched the nylon bag with his foot. 'What's in there?'

'My sleeping-bag and tent.'

'Forget the tent,' he said tersely.

'But——'

'We can both use mine.'

She shot him a startled glance. 'I don't think so.' It was out of the question. Sleep with him? She looked at her mother, but Isobel merely shrugged. She knew what it was like on these expeditions. There was no place for false modesty.

Braden's eyes narrowed angrily. 'I have no intention of carrying anything that is not essential.'

'You won't have to,' she protested strongly. 'I'll carry it myself.'

'Take it out,' he rasped. 'Or don't come.'

Charley had no choice, but her whole body was rigid with resentment as she unzipped the bag and took out the offending tent. She stood up again and faced him, and blue eyes met grey in silent battle.

'Satisfied?' she asked in a tight little voice.

He nodded. 'Let's go.'

She kissed her mother and hugged her tightly, and Isobel shook Braden's hand. There were tears in the woman's eyes. 'Try not to worry too much,' he said to her gently. 'If your husband's to be found, we'll find him.'

'I'll ring you from Lima,' said Charley, her throat tight with emotion. She picked up her bags and followed Braden out to his car. If he had been a gentleman he would have carried them for her, she thought bitterly. But she must remember that they were equals on this mission. He would do her no favours.

It was over an hour's drive to the airport and neither of them spoke very much. Charley was lost in her own thoughts and Braden seemed intent on the road ahead, even though there was not much traffic at this hour in the morning.

They reached Heathrow and checked in, and then there was nothing to do until their flight was called. Once settled into their seats on the plane Charley said, 'Have you managed to find out where my father was heading?'

He nodded. 'Rupert gave me a map, and——'

'Can I see it?' she asked eagerly.

'It's in my case. I'll show you when we get to Lima. We'll stay the night and then take my Cessna to Cuzco where we'll pick up supplies and re-fuel. We'll fly another hundred or so miles in the general direction your father took to save us several days' walking.'

'*Your* Cessna?' Charley queried disbelievingly.

He inclined his head. 'I do a lot of exploring in Peru. It saves me a hell of a lot of time.'

Charley was impressed, though it should not have surprised her. He was probably a millionaire. It was laughable, really, her mother offering him money.

She picked up the in-flight magazine and flicked through it and wished that she were not cushioned between Braden and another giant of a man who occupied the window-seat.

Shoulders jostled shoulders and she could do without this nearness to Braden. She could not deny his magnetism, and it could only get worse.

The fifteen-hour flight had never seemed longer, and Charley felt relief when they finally flew over the Andes and along the narrow desert strip bordering the Pacific Ocean. She had flown to Lima several times before and she looked eagerly for the city crowded into the mouth of the river valley, its outskirts fringed by low sandy moutains.

Jorge Chavez Airport was hot and busy. It took them but a few mintues to go through the passport and Customs checks and make their way outside. To Charley's surprise a car was waiting for them.

The dark-skinned youth driving it grinned widely. *'Buenas tardes, Señor Quest, Señorita.'*

'Buenas tardes, Carlos,' said Braden.

Charley acknowledged his greeting as she climbed into the big, comfortable, air-conditioned car. When they bypassed the city centre she looked at Braden questioningly. 'We're not staying in Lima itself?'

He gave a tiny shake of his head. 'Barranco.'

She frowned.

'Just beyond Miraflores.'

'I know where it is, but why there?'

'Because that's where I live,' he informed her with ill-concealed impatience.

For some reason Charley had assumed she would be staying in a hotel. Though exactly why she had thought this when she had heard him tell her mother that he had a house here, she did not know. It was the obvious place to spend the night. 'I didn't realise,' she said quietly.

'I suppose you're going to tell me next that you don't want to stay there?' he said sharply.

Charley's eyes were cold as she looked at him. He was certainly not making things easy. In fact, he was making it as plain as the nose on his face that he did not want her with him, that he was taking her on sufferance. The whole plane journey had reflected his attitude. He had spoken to her only when necessary. 'Of course I don't mind,' she retorted.

His clear grey eyes held hers for a moment. There was no telling what he was thinking. 'That's good,' he said. 'Not that it would have made any difference. I need to go home. I have things to do before we go searching for your father.'

Charley frowned. 'What sort of things? How long will they take?' Every day was vital so far as she was concerned.

'I hadn't planned on going off again the second I got back to Peru,' he advised her. 'There are several both private and business matters that need to be dealt with. But don't fret, they'll take no more than a few hours. You can go to bed and catch up on your beauty sleep.'

'It's too early,' Charley demurred. With the time difference of six hours between Peru and England, it was only eight o'clock.

Braden shrugged. 'Suit yourself. But as you didn't sleep on the plane and it could be a long time before you see a sprung mattress again, I think you should make the most of it. Personally I can get away with three or four hours. I doubt if you can.'

He was right. She needed at least eight hours' sleep to be any good the next day. She grimaced. 'I'll see.'

They passed the golf course at San Isodro with its surrounding skyscraper apartment blocks and its ultra-modern shopping complexes. They were upmarket now. This was a part of Lima Charley had never had time to explore. She and her father had only ever used the city as a stepping stone to the more exciting undiscovered parts of Peru.

She looked about her with interest as they drove through lively, flashy Miraflores and on to the quieter suburb of Barranco, one of the oldest and most attractive parts of the city, situated above the steep sandy cliffs of the Costa Verda.

Carlos stopped the car in front of one of the many old mansions that were typical of Barranco. This one, set in its own spacious grounds, looked as though it had had a great deal of money spent on it recently, though Charley had time to give it no more than a cursory glance before Braden ushered her inside.

It was cool and spacious and elegant, and they were greeted by a plump, motherly housekeeper with a gap-toothed smile in her dusky face. She looked curiously at Charley as Braden made the introductions, then hurried upstairs to make sure there was a room ready.

Charley lost no time in following her. She was given a large, airy room with an adjoining bathroom, and after a cool, welcoming shower she threw herself down on the bed. She wished with all her heart that Alan Ross had not fallen sick. He was such a nice man, always friendly and open, and she had known him all her life. They would have got on so well together. She was worried enough about her father without having to contend with Braden Quest and his obsessive dislike of her.

A sudden banging on the door made Charley shoot off the bed and pull a towel quickly around her. She frowned at Braden as she opened the door.

'I've brought Rupert's map.' He walked straight in, regardless of her state of undress, and spread it out on the bed. He had changed into a pair of cotton trousers and a thin shirt. His jaw was freshly shaven, his hair damp.

Charley had no choice but to stand beside him and study the sheet of paper, and she could smell the clean freshness of him, and his masculinity, and she felt very vulnerable.

He stabbed his finger at a point somewhere in the middle of the creased piece of paper. 'This is where your father was heading. Here's Cuzco and here's where we'll be landing. We'll make our way along here. I feel certain your father will have——'

'Oh, no,' cut in Charley abruptly. 'He's already covered that ground. I went with him a couple of years ago. I think he would have gone this way.' How she wished she had discussed the trip with her father. If only she hadn't been so insistent it was a wild-goose chase.

Braden looked at her sharply. 'Let's get one thing straight before we start. I'm in charge, and I'm doing this solely for your mother because she's one hell of a worried woman.'

Charley's head jerked. 'You think I'm not?'

'I know you are. I know you think it's your fault. But left to myself I would never have brought you with me. Isobel convinced me that I should—and Alan Ross.'

Charley frowned. 'You spoke to Alan?'

He nodded.

'What did he say?'

'He said I shouldn't misjudge you.' Charley began to smile. 'He also said that you'd probably hold me back.'

Her smile changed to a grim tightening of her mouth. 'Alan said that about me? I don't believe you.'

'He said you're very good—for a woman.'

'I always pulled my weight.'

His smile was cynical. 'I think Alan has a soft spot for you. I practically had to force the truth out of him.'

'And yet you still decided to let me come?'

'It should be quite an experience. Have you ever been to bed with Alan?'

Of all the nerve! Charley's eyes flashed. 'No, I haven't. What made you ask that?'

'Nothing. I just wondered.' His lips quirked. 'You're quite an attractive girl, and out there in the jungle with nothing to do at night, I thought he might have——'

'Well, you thought wrong.' Charley's body bristled with anger. 'And if you lay one finger on me I'll——'

'You'll what?' He clamped his hands on her bare shoulders and grinned wickedly, his fingers biting into her flesh.

'I'll make sure you're in no fit state to touch another woman for a long time,' she grated through her teeth.

'Fighting talk, eh? Maybe this trip will prove more interesting than I thought.' He looked amused by her ferocity.

A frown grooved Charley's brow. 'In what way?'

'In whatever way you like, my fiery friend.'

'If you think I'm going to spend the whole expedition fighting you off, then you'd better think again,' she snapped. 'All I'm concerned with is finding my father.'

'And so am I,' he said gravely, but she could have sworn there was mockery in his dark eyes, and when he let go of her shoulders it was no accident that his hands brushed against the towel. It slid to the floor.

He was there before her, picking it up, holding it out, insolently studying her naked body. Charley went hot all over and grabbed the towel.

'Don't look so embarrassed,' he grinned. 'I don't suppose it will be the last time I see you like this.'

She clenched her teeth and glared. 'If I have anything to do with it, it will.' Did he really think she would undress in front of him? She would sleep in her clothes if necessary. She felt on fire. No other man had succeeded in making her feel so aware of

her own body. She had always been one of them.
Now Braden Quest was making it perfectly clear she
was all woman.

'Would you mind leaving the room so that I can get
dressed?' she asked tightly.

His brows rose. 'We haven't finished discussing
which route we should take.' And he bent down
again over the map.

Charley was compelled to fix the towel and stand
by him, and this time she knew he was deliberately
goading her. His arm touched hers, sending tiny
quivers of sensation through her limbs, and he
constantly turned his head to ask her questions, and
the question in his eyes was nothing like the one on
his lips.

'Having met your father,' he said, when once again
Charley had disagreed with his suggestion, 'I'm
positive he would have gone this way. He has a very
logical mind and——'

'You actually remember meeting my father?' she
interrupted with surprise. Braden must have met so
many people during the course of his work that it was
highly unlikely he would recall one man.

'Yes,' he admitted. 'I didn't at first, I must confess,
not until I got talking to Alan. It was actually Alan
who introduced him to me at an international
anthropological conference in Ecuador. Your father
showed a very keen interest in the Inca culture. We
spent quite a time comparing notes.'

Charley nodded. 'I remember when he came home
he never stopped talking about you. You made quite
an impression.'

'But not the same impression on his daughter? I'm
surprised he didn't tell me about you, since you seem
to share his love of the Incas. I would have been most

interested to hear about his daughter who thinks she's a boy. It amazes me you haven't cropped your hair short.' He reached out and caught a handful of her thick black locks, pulling her mercilessly towards him.

'Blame my father, not me, for the way I am,' she rasped, trying to snatch free, but succeeding only in hurting herself. 'He wanted a boy. He's encouraged me to follow in his footsteps.'

And suddenly her face was only centimetres away from his and his eyes were on her mouth and she thought he was going to kiss her. Quite unconsciously the tip of her tongue moistened her lips and she stopped breathing and she could not keep wondering what it would be like to be kissed by this man.

Then just as abruptly he let her go and marched across to the window, looking out at the ocean far below. There was a new harshness to his face, and Charley wondered why. Had she been wrong in supposing he was going to kiss her?

Actually she was glad he hadn't, because it would have made things difficult. He had a fatal fascination for her whether she liked it or not, and it would be madness to complicate their relationship by sexual desire.

'We'll discuss the situation again over dinner,' he said tersely, swinging round and looking at her. 'I have several phone calls to make, supplies to order, et cetera. I want them to be ready and waiting when we get to Cuzco.'

'I'd like to help,' she said. 'I always helped my father decide what we'd need.'

His eyes were cold as they bit into hers. 'I am not your father. If I were I'd never have let you get involved in any of this.'

Charley glared at him mutinously.'What are you, a male chauvinist? Do you believe a woman's place is in the home?'

His eyes narrowed as he walked towards her. 'I have no objection to a woman having a career.'

'But you don't think archaeology is one of them?'

'Not at all, archaeology is a very fine profession. But searching tropical jungles when you have neither the stamina nor the build for it is sheer foolhardiness.'

Charley gasped. 'I don't think I've done badly so far.'

'With a doting father to pave the way, I'm not surprised.'

'My father did not make things easy for me,' she protested. 'I got no favours.'

He looked at her for several long seconds. 'And you'll get none from me.'

Her chin rose. 'I don't expect any.'

He nodded. 'So long as we understand one another . . .'

'Perfectly.'

Braden picked up the map and left the room. Charley was furiously angry. How dared he speak to her like that? He really was the most aggravating man she had ever met. She lay down on the bed, and the next thing she knew he was hammering on her door, announcing that it was time for dinner.

She dressed in the same blouse and trousers, and after brushing her hair joined Braden in the dining-room. Her face was bare of make-up. She had brought none with her. There would be no time for that sort of thing. Insect repellent would be the order of the day.

'I've been talking to someone who was with Spencer the day he left,' he informed her after a few minutes.

Charley looked up from the spoonful of avocado

she was about to put into her mouth. What a stroke of luck! 'Who?'

'Robert Kinsey, an old friend of mine from the anthropological museum.'

'Did he say which way my father went?'

Braden nodded, and his lips quivered with amusement. 'You're not going to like this, Charley. It was the way I first suggested.'

She hated the way he was laughing at her, but she merely shrugged and smiled. 'So long as we know, I don't care.'

'Really?' he mocked.

'Really,' she confirmed. 'Has he any news? Has he heard anything since my father left?'

'I'm afraid not.'

'Did my father go alone?'

'No, he took an Indian who came down from the mountains a few years ago and is now more or less civilised, and a mestizo youth of about twenty. They've both apparently been on this sort of expedition before.'

'And has either of them returned?'

'I've no idea.'

Charley carried on eating for a moment, then she said, 'What's your honest opinion? Do you think my father's alive?'

He thought carefully before answering. 'From all accounts, Spencer's a very experienced man. He wouldn't take unnecessary risks. But you and I both know that deep in the jungle there are tribes who do not welcome the white man.'

Charley nodded her agreement.

'And who can blame them?' His tone suddenly changed. 'First the conquistadors drove them out of their homes, and now the oil corporations and the lumber companies, to say nothing of settlers and

missionaries who are forcing through land-title agree-
ments to which they have no conceivable right.'
Braden's voice vibrated with anger. This was
obviously a subject on which he had strong feelings.
'Your father could have met a hostile tribe. Anything
could have happened to him.' He paused a moment.
'Although somehow I don't think so.'

'I hope not,' breathed Charley. She could not bear
the thought of her father dying in this manner.

'Or he could have fallen ill—that's always a very
strong possibility. Medical kits aren't much help if
you get appendicitis.'

'My father's never ill,' she protested.

'The third alternative is that he's simply been
detained by a group of Indians. I think this is the
most likely.'

Charley's eyes widened. 'Why would they do that?
We've met plenty of Indians on our travels, some
friendly, some wary and suspicious, some definitely
hostile, but they've never kept us prisoner. My father
speaks a little of their language. He's always
managed to persuade them that we mean no harm.'

'Not a prisoner, exactly,' said Braden. 'But there's a
group of Indians living in the region Spencer is exploring who for years have had in their midst a white
man. A doctor who once cured a very sick and very
important member of their tribe. Their own witch
doctor had been unable to do anything and they
thought it a miracle. They invited him to stay and live
with them.'

'And he did?' asked Charley incredulously.

Braden nodded. 'He had no family and he rather
liked the idea of getting away from civilsation. He
died last year.'

'And you think they asked my father to take his

place? What good would that do? He knows a little bit about medicine, but not much.'

'I don't know,' said Braden. 'It's just a theory.'

She shook her head, fear making her angry. 'My father would never stay.'

'Have you any better suggestions?'

'Yes, that's he's found the lost city, and time has no meaning.'

Braden tossed his head scornfully.

But Charley could not accept that her father was living with the Indians. He had a home and a family whom he loved. He wouldn't do this unless it was against his will. She swallowed with difficulty. 'Do you know where these Indians live?'

Braden nodded.

'Have you met them?' If they trusted Braden, then maybe they would release her father. And what was she doing thinking there was any truth in what he said? Damn the man!

'Once. I didn't find them very friendly. They're more suspicious than most. It's rare anyone travels so deep into the jungle.'

'So if they're holding my father prisoner they're hardly likely to listen to you, or me? They might even—kill us?' Her eyes widened with horror. In all the years she had been accompanying her father she had never encountered anything like this.

Braden fingered the scar on his cheek and she looked at him aghast.

'Did the Indians do that?'

He seemed to take a long time in answering, and Charley's imagination worked overtime. It had never occured to her it would be this dangerous. Why hadn't she let Braden go alone? She would be no match for a hostile Indian.

And when he finally nodded she nearly died. 'Oh, my God!'

Then he grinned. 'It was my own fault. We had a friendly fight and I lost.'

'Friendly? What was he using, a machete?'

'Actually we were using our fists,' he admitted. 'He tripped me and I fell and smashed my face on the edge of a stone.'

Charley shuddered. 'Were you far from civilisation?'

'Several days away,' he shrugged.

'So what did you do?'

'Slapped a plaster on it and hoped for the best. If I'd had it stitched straight away it might not have been so ugly. Do you find it off-putting?'

'No,' she answered truthfully. 'As a matter of fact I think it does something for you. It makes you look as though you'd led a wickedly interesting life.'

'Which I have—interesting, anyway. I don't know about wicked.' But there was a gleam in his eyes as he spoke.

'I'm still worried about my father,' she said. 'I wish you hadn't said anything.'

'You did ask.'

She nodded and pushed her plate away. 'I don't want anything else to eat.'

'Juanita will be mortally offended. She's prepared *pescado a la chorillana.* Surely a little fish won't be hard to swallow? Besides, you can't afford not to eat properly.'

Charley saw the sense in what he said and managed to eat most of what was put before her. They washed it down with a bottle of local wine and afterwards, much to her disgust, Charley felt ready for bed.

Braden still had work to do, but he warned her that he wanted to be away early the next morning.

Charley set her wristwatch alarm and when she awoke took a long, luxurious shower—the last one she would have for goodness knew how long—and then dressed in cotton trousers and a bush shirt, braiding her hair and pinning it on top of her head. When Braden tapped on her door she was ready.

He looked at her long and hard. 'The testing time has almost arrived,' he said. No comment on her appearance, whether he approved or otherwise. With her hair up she looked less like a girl and more like a boy, but even so, compared to Braden, she was still essentially feminine.

He in his turn looked if possible tougher than ever in a pair of khaki trousers and a matching shirt, his hair damp and closely following the shape of his head.

She eyed the scar and had a sudden inexplicable urge to touch it. She would have liked him to hold her close and reassure her that no matter what happened, what difficulties they encountered, he would always be there to help and guide and protect. But that would never be the case. She was on her own. *The testing time*, he had said, and it would be up to her to prove that she was as good as she had made out.

CHAPTER THREE

AFTER breakfast Carlos drove them to the airport where Braden's Cessna was ready and waiting. Charley had been in small planes before. Her father sometimes hired one, complete with pilot, naturally. But never had she felt so conscious of being alone in the universe. There was just herself and Braden. Whatever happpened now, she was in the hands of this merciless man.

It took them six hours to reach Cuzco, a beautiful bustling colonial city, the ancient heart of the Inca empire, and much more interesting than Lima itself. But today they were not exploring. The supplies Braden had ordered were ready and waiting, and after loading and re-fuelling they set off again on the next leg of their journey.

They flew over the ruins of Machu Picchu, the most important, or certainly the most exploited, Inca site in Peru, and finally, after over an hour's flying, they prepared to land. The jungle, which had been nothing more than a dense dull grey-green from three thousand feet, resolved into individual trees and branches as they lost height. They landed in a small field, bounching to a halt a short distance away from the curtain of jungle.

Immediately the plane was surrounded by about a dozen grinning Indians all clamouring to shake Braden's hand, the children eagerly accepting the toffees he handed to them. He was clearly well known and much liked, and spoke fluently in their language.

Charley herself was viewed with suspicion until one of the half-naked men asked Braden a question. Looking at her with a fond smile, he put his arm about her shoulders and rattled something off in Quechua.

Immediately they all wanted to shake her hand too, grinning and looking knowingly from one to the other.

'What did you say?' asked Charley suspiciously.

His expression was perfectly serious. 'That you're my wife.'

Charley gasped. 'Why?'

'Because they will accept you more readily.'

'Wouldn't they have accepted me if you'd told them the truth?'

'That I'd brought you against my will? This way we'll get extra special treatment. I'm relying on them to lend us a mule and perhaps one of their youths. The jungle is very dense the way we're going, and somehow I don't think you'll be much use to me.' There was again that disparaging tone in his voice which he had used when they first met.

Charley was quick to anger. 'You won't give me a chance, will you?'

He quirked a brow. 'Don't worry, your chance will come. It will be interesting to see what you're made of.'

'Tougher stuff than you give me credit for,' she spat.

'I think you'd better smile if we're to convince these people that we're in love.' Pulling her to him, he turned up her face and kissed her. 'Don't you dare struggle,' he mouthed softly as he felt her stiffen. 'Act the part even though it kills you.'

Charley found she had no need to pretend. The

hours spent together had increased the awareness
she had already felt and tried to deny. She could
ignore his magnetism no longer. She accepted the
kiss willingly, feeling desire course through her, and
her arms went involuntarily around him.

When he thought the kiss had gone on long
enough Braden held her at arm's length and looked
deep into her eyes. 'Quite an act.'

Charley turned away and saw the circle of grinning
onlookers and self-consciously pulled out of his
grasp.

'I think you've convinced them. In fact——' his tone
lowered conspiratorially '—you almost convinced
me.' Charley's eyes flashed her contempt, and he
laughed. 'Let's go and see what sort of a deal we can
do.'

The Indian settlement consisted of several wooden
huts with thatched roofs, and they were shown to a
hut which was normally used to store maize, but
which was almost empty at this moment. They were
told that if they so wished they could spend the night
there.

Charely had not realised they would be staying;
she had thought they would begin their journey
straight away. When she glanced at her watch,
however, she discovered to her surprise that it was
already early evening. But sharing a hut with
Braden . . .?

It's no different from sharing his tent, a tiny voice
said inside her. In fact, it wouldn't be so confined.
She might as well get used to the fact that from now
on she would be living as close to Braden as if they
were indeed man and wife. She changed her expression to a smile. 'I'll get the sleeping-bags.'

And while Braden talked with the Indians she

unloaded the plane, stacking everything into a corner of the hut, their sleeping-bags on top ready to lay out on the dirt floor later. Darkness fell while she worked. She was used to the rapid change from daylight to total blackness.

They were invited to share a meal of maize bread and fish, which was surprisingly tasty, but Braden made instant coffee from their supplies rather than drink the very strong brew the Indians preferred.

Charley went to bed early, hoping to be asleep before Braden joined her, but the moment she switched off her torch she heard the patter of tiny feet. Turning it on again, she sat up in a sweat as she saw a rat run into a pile of maize, and resolved that this was the last time she would sleep anywhere except in the tent, tightly zipped to keep out intruders. It was not so much that she was afraid of rodents, or any animal or insect for that matter, but she did not like the thought of them running over her while she slept.

When Braden eventually joined her, Charley pretended to be asleep, listening as he spread his own bag on the floor, acutely conscious of the intimacy of their sharing the hut. He fell asleep almost immediately and after that Charley slept also, not stirring until Braden shook her by the shoulder.

'Wake up,' he said brusquely. 'It's time we were on our way.' He was already dressed and once he had assured himself that she was properly awake he disappeared.

This was the true beginning of their search, thought Charley. Apprehension knotted her stomach as she scrambled out of her bag and washed in a bowl of water brought to her by one of the Indian women. Next she liberally sprayed herself with insect repellent.

Above what was called the insect line, about four

thousand feet above sea level, there were no mosquitoes or other insects, but until they climbed higher Charley knew they would be a real menace. She also took a dose of Vitamin B, something that her father had always insisted she do. He said it made your skin smell so horrible that the mosquitoes could not face the thought of landing.

By seven they were on their way, accompanied by a mule laden with their supplies and two Indian youths. Charley brought up the rear.

The jungle here was dense and comparatively cool, which was very welcome after the intense heat. It consisted of three distinct layers. The tallest trees were the vast silk cotton, below them thorny bamboo and small palms and softwoods, and then the dense underbrush of ferns and stinging nettles, seedlings and bushes.

For a couple of hours they followed a narrow path, and Charley's legs began to ache as she kept resolutely up with them. Then suddenly they came out into sunlight so brilliant that it hurt her eyes. They paused for a few minutes' rest, even though Coyaso and Jorge looked as though they could go on for ever. Charley wondered whether it was for her benefit.

Braden stood frowning into the distance, his hand shading his eyes from the sun. They were in a valley and the river had dried out to a couple of metres so they would be able to walk easily along the riverbed. 'Your father followed this same path,' he told her. 'He actually slept in the same hut we used last night.'

Charley's eyes widened and a little niggle of annoyance shot through her. 'Thank you for telling me earlier.'

'What good would it have done? Can you speak

Quechua? Could you have asked the Indians any questions?'

'No, but——'

'So I'm telling you now that he went this way.'

'Did they know exactly where he was heading?'

He shook his head. 'Unfortunately not. But they don't think any harm will have befallen him.'

'How can they be so sure?'

'They can't,' he admitted

Which did not help Charley's peace of mind. She walked away from him and cupped her hands beneath a stream which trickled down the mountainside. The water was wonderfully cool and refreshing. 'Let's press on,' she said.

The next time they stopped it was for lunch, and by then Charley was feeling the strain, though she was determined not to show it. Braden had not once asked if she was all right. What a hateful man he was.

The Indians lit a fire and they soon had hot water to mix with their powdered soup. They ate maize bread and cheese, and drank coffee, and Charley felt better.

But soon they were off again. Her father had never set such a crippling pace. Maybe he *had* made allowances for her, though she had never been aware of it. She had always congratulated herself on keeping up. Perhaps it was because of her father's age that he went slower. Braden was younger and stronger and physically fitter, but she knew one thing, she would never be able to keep up this pace day after day.

Just before dusk they made camp for the night, and Charley felt reasonably pleased with her performance. Admittedly, they had been following the riverbed for several kilometres, but even so it was not all easy going. Once or twice she had caught Braden's eyes on her, but she had given no indication that she was struggling. It was what he expected and possibly the reason he was pushing her so hard. Her resentment of him increased by the hour.

Again they cooked a meal over the fire, and by the time they had eaten Charley was ready to drop on her feet. 'Goodnight,' she mumbled, and zipped herself into the tent.

She crawled into her sleeping-bag fully dressed and was in that nebulous state between wakefulness and sleep when Braden decided to join her. Immediately she was wide awake, and when his hand touched her shoulder she shot up to look at him. In the glow from his torch, his face looked dark and threatening and inside the bag her fists clenched.

'Why are you still wearing your clothes?' he wanted to know.

'Because I want to, because I feel——'

'Safer?' he suggested mockingly. 'Don't worry, I have no designs on your body.'

'Not from you,' she protested. 'From creepy-crawlies and mosquitoes.'

'They won't get in here,' he derided. 'Don't bother to lie. It's me you're afraid of, isn't it?' He began stripping off his shirt.

'It might be,' she answered, her eyes defensive.

'Look,' he said, 'let's get this straight right here and now. Making love to you is the furthest thought from my mind.'

In other words he was not attracted to her, thought Charley perversely. Which made her awareness of him all the more difficult to handle.

'And once we reach higher altitudes where the air is thinner, my sex drive will be virtually nil. I'm sure you must know that.' Charley shrugged with pretended indifference. 'It doesn't bother you?' There was the vestige of a smile on his lips.

'I prefer it.'

'I was forgetting,' he mocked, 'that you think of yourself as a boy. You wouldn't be interested in me.' And it seemed to her then that he deliberately unzipped his trousers.

He wore black, close-fitting briefs and he stood there proud and tall and looked down at her. 'I suggest you get undressed, too. You'll sleep more comfortably.'

'I will, when you're in bed.'

'You don't want me looking at you?'

No, she didn't but she would not tell him that. 'There's not enough room for the two of us to move about.'

'Oh, I'm sorry,' he jeered, and sat down cross-legged on top of his sleeping-bag. 'OK now?'

'Damn you!' hissed Charley through her teeth, but nevertheless she got up and took off her shirt and trousers, eyeing him boldly as she did so, waiting for him to give himself away by the merest flicker of an eyelid. But it was as if he were carved out of stone. Not even the fact that she was bra-less seemed to affect him. And not until she crawled into her bag and turned her back on him did he speak again.

'Might I say that you don't—look like a boy. In fact——'

But Charley had had enough. 'I don't want to hear what you think,' she cut in coldly. 'I want to go to sleep.'

'Do you think you will sleep—worrying about what I might do to you?' The mockery was still there.

'I shall try,' she answered stiffly.

'Good, because you'll need a good night's rest. I'm

hoping to cover much more ground tomorrow.'

Charley silently groaned. It had taken all her energy to keep up today. If he went any faster she would never manage it. She heard him climb into his sleeping-bag and ventured to turn her head to peep at him. About one metre separated them, and Charley could not dismiss her apprehension about being cocooned inside this canvas tent with a virtual stranger.

When she had written to Braden for help she had not envisaged any of this. He had completely turned the tables, taking charge when she would have preferred to do the leading herself. Maybe it was right that she should bow before his superiority, but after all it was *her* father they were looking for, so why shouldn't she have some say in what they did and which way they went?

It was a long time before she slept, and it seemed as though she had only just shut her eyes before he was roughly waking her. 'Get up,' he said, 'we're ready to move.'

He was already dressed and freshly shaven, his sleeping-bag neatly rolled. Charley waited until he had left the tent then pulled on her shirt and trousers, wishing he had roused her earlier, wishing in fact that she had woken herself. Glancing at her watch she saw that it was only just after six. No wonder she felt tired.

But he had exaggerated when he had said they were ready. A pot of coffee was bubbling on the fire which had been renewed from last night's embers and, after she had found a mountain stream in which to wash, Charley drank two cups and ate some more of the delicious soup, feeling immediately better.

Within half an hour they had resumed their

Within half an hour they had resumed their journey, and during the following four days they crossed valleys and rivers and climbed steep, rocky hillsides, and despite blisters on her feet Charley strode heroically on. Braden treated her no differently from how he would have done had she been a man, and she kept her aches and pains to herself. It was a gruelling pace, but if it meant they would find her father sooner then she would grit her teeth and keep up.

They occasionally met an isolated group of Indians, when they would exchange a few words and perhaps purchase more maize for the mule and bread for themselves. Sometimes it was easy going, but sometimes they had to hack their way through trails and heave great boulders from their path.

The two Indians did most of the hard work, but Braden was not slow to help. He never handed Charley a machete, though, not after the first time when she had insisted on helping and the Indians had fallen about in a heap laughing at her efforts. Personally she thought she had done pretty well, her father would certainly have commended her, but not Braden. He had given her a look enough to kill, plucked the knife from her hand, and never suggested she take her turn again.

'My father couldn't have come this way,' Charley protested, the first time they cut their way through virgin jungle.

Braden looked at her derisively. 'It's impossible to follow the exact same trail, as you well know. There are so many different routes he could have taken.'

'But what if we miss him?'

'We shan't,' he said tersely. 'A white man is known to have passed through the village the other

side of that range some weeks ago. It was probably
your father.'

Again this was something he had not told her.
Charley felt her anger grow. 'And you didn't think it
of sufficient importance to tell me?'

'I can't be sure it was him, but Robert Kinsey told
me that he knows of no other expedition at this
moment. So it's highly likely. Calm down, Charley. If
I have any real news, I'll tell you at once.'

Charley continued to glare.

'You have beautiful eyes, especially when you're
angry,' he said with an insolent smile. 'You remind
me of a wild cat; a puma, perhaps.'

'And I can assure you I have claws like a cat if I get
riled,' she spat.

'Then I must remember to keep out of your way.'

The thought that her father had been seen not too
far ahead spurred Charley to extra effort. The track
ascended tortuously now. They were above the insect
line, which was one blessing, but the rare
atmosphere sapped her energy. She chewed some
coca leaves and managed to keep up.

Coca, she had been told by her father many years
ago, was vital to the well-being of people living in these
high altitudes. It had always been an important part of
the Inca diet, and even the Indians living high in the
Andes today still chewed coca. It helped combat breath-
lessness and provided energy to undertake physical
challenges. Taken raw it was not a dangerous drug, but
it was nevertheless the basic ingredient for cocaine and
there was a thriving market for it.

Charley was feeling pretty pleased with herself
until Braden decided to make a detour along a narrow
footpath cut into the rockface. 'I want to take a look at
some Inca ruins,' he announced.

Charley thought it a pretty odd time to be exploring, and felt sure he was deliberately testing her, so wisely held her tongue. They tethered the mule and followed the track, and there was a sheer drop below them. It was like walking along a windowsill on the top floor of a high building. Charley was overcome by the worst attack of vertigo she had ever experienced.

But not for anything would she admit defeat. She told herself it was purely psychological, took a deep breath, and turning her face to the wall proceeded sideways like a crab, clutching desperately at small plants growing out of cracks in the surface, not daring to look down. Just once she turned, and the whole of the canyon leapt up at her.

The Incas, she knew, rarely travelled in the valleys, always laying out their roads half-way up the mountainsides, and this must have been one of their tracks.

Neither the Indians nor Braden had the slightest fear of heights, and as they waited for her to catch up she felt their impatience. Her father would never have insisted she make such a hazardous climb, he would have found an easier route. She had never realised until now how much he had protected her and she dared not think about the return journey.

But if she expected Braden to congratulate her then she was mistaken. He waited until she was safely on the wider footpath up to the plateau, then he forged on ahead. Charley felt angry tears prick the backs of her eyes, which was unusual for her. What a beast the man was! He could at least have offered her some word of praise.

Soon they were standing in what had once been a huge courtyard, in the middle of which were temple ruins. There were the remains of a circular stone wall, and in the centre of that was a huge, flat, solid rock about two metres high with shallow channels running from each corner.

'A sacrificial altar,' announced Braden with some satisfaction, looking directly at Charley. 'And they didn't only sacrifice animals.' He ran his fingers along the channels where the hapless creatures' legs would be tied. 'The victims were sometimes virgins.'

Charley knew all about this, but even so she shuddered. Braden seemed to be insinuating that he would like to tie her down here. Not to kill her, just to see what sort of a reaction he would get. He wanted her at his mercy. He still didn't approve of her accompanying him and he was doing his very best to make things difficult for her—both mentally and physically.

He ran his fingers into a hollow at one end of the altar. 'Do you know what this is?'

She nodded. 'It's to catch the victim's blood after her heart's been cut out.'

'And then it's left as an offering to Inti,' he finished for her.

'The Sun God,' she confirmed. 'What a barbarous custom.'

'And yet it fascinates you?'

She nodded. 'The Incas always have.'

'To such an extent that you'd risk life and limb to see the places where they once lived? Not many girls would do that. It would be sufficient to read about them.' Was that a compliment? Charley doubted it. 'And not many men would take their daughters with them,' he added pointedly. 'They would think more of their safety.'

Her chin shot up. 'Are you saying my father was in the wrong?'

Braden shrugged. 'It was his choice, although I know

I wouldn't let any daughter of mine do it.'

'My father never led me into danger. I never had any mishaps.'

'Then you were lucky.'

'Or perhaps my father is more careful than you give him credit for,' she tossed angrily.

'So why is he missing now?'

Charley's blue eyes were full of aggression. 'You gave me your opinion on that. And if you're right, then it's nothing to do with expertise. Have we seen all you want to see? I think we ought to be on our way.'

Braden glanced at his watch. 'It will soon be dark. We'll go back and make camp for the night.'

Charley could not believe the day had passed so quickly. Time was flying and she was amazing herself with her resilience. Braden did not pause for rests so often as her father used to, and by the end of each day she was thoroughly exhausted, though she never admitted it. She was pushing herself to her limits, the thought of proving to Braden that she was made of tougher material then she looked spurring her on.

Across the gorge, on a much bigger plateau, they could see more remains which had not been visible from lower down. 'That would be the city,' announced Braden, 'and there would have been a suspension bridge across here.'

Charley wished there was a bridge now so that she did not have to negotiate that fearful track again. It looked much easier to climb down the mountain over there. But somehow, by sheer stubbornness and determination to prove to Braden that she could do anything he could do, she made it, although by the time she got to the bottom her legs were so weak she could hardly stand.

But she was given no peace. 'Don't sit down,' he

rasped, pausing in his act of putting up the tent. 'It's your turn to cook.'

Charley could not believe it. Had he no idea of the state she was in? But she would not argue. She would do it if it killed her. Jorge and Coyaso had already collected a heap of twigs for the fire.

She fetched water from the waterfall that cascaded a few metres away and soon had a pot boiling into which she added powdered stew. They ate it with thick chunks of maize bread and followed it with bananas and oranges they had purchased from the last group of Indians. Strong coffee finished the meal, and afterwards they sat talking around the fire.

It was much colder at this altitude and Charley was glad of its warmth, but soon she felt her eyes beginning to shut and she took herself off to bed. She had become used now to sharing with Braden, and as she crawled tiredly into her sleeping-bag she gave no thought at all to the fact that he would soon be joining her.

For once she woke before him. Carefully unzipping the tent, she stepped outside. Day was about to break. The sun was ready to push back the velvet darkness of night. All she could hear was the rush of water and the faint rustling of leaves. The Indians were asleep on the floor by the grey ash of the fire. Charley headed for the waterfall.

She stripped off and stood beneath the icy waters. It took her breath away, but it was good so good, so invigorating, the first proper wash she'd had since they had left Lima. She closed her eyes and turned her face up to the teeming water. It was heaven, sheer bliss. She let it pour over her, and when she opened her eyes again Braden stood beside her, most of his clothing discarded.

Charley froze. He had followed her! He must have

been awake all the time, and done this deliberately to annoy her. 'Can't you respect my need for privacy?' she snapped, stepping back a pace to avoid the heaviest of the water. It was now like a liquid curtain between them and she could not see his face clearly, but she could tell that he was grinning and enjoying her discomfort.

'I thought you'd got over your shyness. I've not noticed it troubling you lately.'

'There's no point, is there?' she scorned. 'Otherwise I'd never get any sleep.'

'You look like a child when you're asleep, did you know that? Your face goes all soft and relaxed, and there's none of the aggression that's usually there when you're speaking to me.'

Charley stared at him in in disbelief. 'You watch me?' The thought brought a prickly heat to her skin, despite the coldness of the water.

'Quite frequently. It's such a novelty—having a girl share my tent.'

'I hope it doesn't mean you're getting any ideas.'

'I can't believe you're as immune to me as you make out.' He stepped closer towards her and Charley would have backed had there been anywhere to go, but there was a wall of sheer rock behind her.

She looked at him with as much dignity as she could muster. 'Are you thinking of putting your theory to the test? I wouldn't recommend it. I can fight like a tiger if I need to.'

'I'm well aware of that,' he said, but he was still smiling and he was still moving towards her. 'Do you know the reason why the Incas always built their cities close to waterfalls?'

Charley nodded. 'Because they believed the running water purified their souls.'

'And is that what you're trying to do, purify your soul? Or is it perhaps your natural desires you're trying to quell? It's very cold, isn't it? I'm surprised you're staying under so long.'

'If you moved, I would go.'

He spread his hands. 'I'm not stopping you.'

But she would have to walk past him! It was either that, though, or stay here and argue, and she was getting colder by the minute.

With a supreme effort of will she held her head high and walked through the cascading water. Suddenly his hand shot out and he caught her arm, pulling her towards him, their bodies not quite touching but near enough for her to be aware of his near-nakedness, and of his overpowering masculinity that she had fought so hard to resist.

'You're some woman, Charley,' he said, much to her surprise. 'You were terrified on that mountain yesterday, weren't you? But not so much as a whisper of fear left your lips.' Coming from him, that was a compliment indeed. 'But you can't be all hard and tough, even though you're doing your best to let me think so. There has to be a soft inner core.'

'And you think that taking me against my will will help you find it?' she asked coldly.

'I wouldn't do that. I've never in all my life kissed a woman against her will.' Still holding her wrist, he touched a finger to her chin, then ran his thumb softly over her lips, sending a thousand sensations swimming through Charley's veins.

She ought to move, she knew that, but the combination of the running water and Braden's deliberately sensual voice was having an effect on her over which she had no control. It was as though they were alone in the world, in the whole universe, and imperceptibly she drew closer to him until, with a jolt like a thousand volts, their bodies touched.

His was cool and hard, and yet set her on fire. There was something erotic about standing beneath this curtain of silver, and when his head moved towards hers her lips parted of their own volition.

The whole world spun about her head as his kiss deepened and his hands urged her body even closer. One tiny sane corner of her mind told her that this was wrong, that there was no time on an expedition of this kind for making love. She was searching for her missing father, for heaven's sake! But the longer the kiss went on, the more common sense deserted her.

She could feel the whole pulsing length of his body against hers, and her heart beat as frantically as it had on the cliff-face yesterday afternoon. The noise of the water filled her ears, and just when she thought she could stand the excitement no longer Braden let her go.

'As I thought,' he said mockingly, 'the lady is no different from anyone else, no matter how loudly she protests.' Clearly the experience had not been so devastating for him.

Charley answered by slapping him angrily across the face, but his laugh followed her all the way back to camp.

CHAPTER FOUR

CHARLEY found it impossible to ignore the feelings Braden had aroused inside her beneath the waterfall. Sitting around the camp fire for breakfast she tried not to look at him, but against her will her eyes were drawn in his direction.

A secret smile played about his lips, almost a triumphant smile, and she would have given her eye teeth to know what he was thinking. Perhaps he had been expecting her to respond to him—and she had not let him down. Nor was she failing him now. It was a disquieting thought.

Did he know that when their eyes met her senses quickened? She did not want to be attracted to him, but she could not help herself. It was something over which she had no control. He had an indefinable magnetism that surely every woman must feel and respond to.

It was a relief when breakfast was over and she could help pack their equipment. Yet even though her hands were occupied she was still vitally aware of Braden and realised the danger she had placed herself in. From now on there would be a subtle difference in their relationship—at least so far as she was concerned.

What Braden felt she did not know. The kiss had probably meant nothing to him. In fact, she knew it hadn't. The whole incident had been stage-managed. He had set out to see what sort of a reaction he would get—and she had not disappointed him.

They began their day's trek at a crippling pace, the two Indians hacking a pathway through scrub and bushes, wielding their machetes with ease born of practice. Yet even the effort of walking in this rare atmosphere soaked Charley with perspiration and made her gasp for each breath.

If she had thought Braden would be more lenient towards her now, she was mistaken. Whatever the kiss meant, it had broken no barriers. He was still treating her as an equal, expecting her to keep up with them without any complaints, and, while this was what she had wanted in the beginning, Charley now began to feel a perverse irritation that he was not making any allowances.

They came to a point where stepping-stones led across a river. The stones had, decided Charley, as she stepped from one to another, been placed here at some time by human hand—they were too precise to be an act of nature. Her father would have given her a hand, or at the very least made sure she could manage, but not Braden. He strode on ahead and not once did she see him look back. She could have slipped and knocked herself out for all the interest he was taking. Her blood reached boiling point, as it had so often done during these last few days.

On the northern side of the river was a stone path which made the going easier. It was an old Inca track, each stone individually shaped and fitted to form a smooth surface. As always, Charley was impressed by their methods of construction. Their houses and temples were built in the same manner and never ceased to amaze her.

This particular track was about two metres wide, enough for two men, or one man and his llama, and Charley thrilled anew at the thought of walking in the footsteps of the legendary Incas of four hundred years ago. She would have liked to talk to Braden about it but, as usual, he was stalking ahead.

They stopped for lunch and then headed on again through areas of fairly thick undergrowth and other places where it was much less overgrown. On one occasion Braden actually took the time to point out to her the stone ruins of some houses. 'Probably farmers,' he said, 'who retreated deeper into the jungle when the Spaniards came looking for gold.' His lips compressed for a moment. 'Do you realise, Charley, that in twenty years from now the Indian tribes may cease to exist in any meaningful way?'

'Things are that bad?' she frowned.

'The Indians are being deprived of their rights,' he said fiercely. 'They are being deceived and insulted, and because of this some of them are actually going to the large towns and trying to hide their origins. It's criminal they should feel the need to do this.'

He felt deeply for these people and Charley was inclined to agree with him. It was a shame these harmless Indians couldn't be left alone. And they *were* harmless. It was only when they were trying to defend their own land that they attacked.

All the time they were climbing higher and higher. When they finally stopped for the night they lit a fire and ate their supper, and Charley went early to bed. She ached in every limb and thought longingly of a hot bath and a sprung mattress.

When Braden joined her she was still awake. More often than not, since that first night when he had made her undress in front of him, she was asleep before he turned in. But tonight she could feel again his mouth on hers and just thinking about it sent a dizzying spiral of desire through her body, and sleep was the furthest thought from her mind.

Now he was here and she kept her eyes tight closed in case he saw what she was feeling. She heard the faint rustle as he took off his shirt, and the sound of the zip on his trousers being lowered, then him hopping from one leg to the other as he took them off. When he should have been wriggling into his sleeping-bag, all was silent. Charley could stand it no longer. She carefully opened one eye—and discovered that he was watching her.

'I knew you weren't asleep,' he jeered, a faint smile on his lips.

'But I soon shall be,' she said, turning her back on him. Why was he interested in whether she was awake or not? Did he intend to kiss her again? Her heart raced at the very thought.

'What's keeping you awake? It's been a gruelling day, I thought you'd flake out.'

Charley chose not to answer.

'Has it anything to do with what happened this morning?'

'No,' she answered, her voice muffled by the sleeping-bag which she had pulled around her face.

'Little liar!'

Charley tensed and felt sure he would notice. He seemed not to miss one tiny little thing, except when she was struggling to keep up. Or was that deliberate? Somehow she thought it might be.

'You're quite safe.' There was an odd inflection in his voice that she had not heard before. 'I lapsed this morning, I went against my own code. I shan't touch you again.'

Which must mean that the experience had done nothing for him! Charley's lips clamped and she felt strangely hurt. Why was it that this man made her feel vulnerable when it had never happened before? No one had ever made her feel even remotely like this.

He climbed into his sleeping-bag and she heard him wriggling about until finally he settled, but it was a long time before Charley slept, and again she woke before dawn had broken. Only this time something had disturbed her and she was not sure what it was. Her first instinct was to glance at Braden, but so far as she could make out in the shadowy darkness of the tent he was fast asleep.

Then she heard it again, a soft growl outside, and the hairs on the back of her neck rose. It was the first time in all the years she had spent travelling that she had heard an animal so close to their sleeping-quarters. Her father had taught her that no wild animal would harm them unless provoked, but that did not make her feel any easier. What was it? What was he doing? Was he after scraps of food? And how about Coyaso and Jorge sleeping beneath the stars? Would the animal harm them? Charley went quite cold.

'Braden,' she whispered, almost afraid to make a sound in case the creature heard and came to investigate. It would be a simple matter for him to slash the tent open with his claws. She broke out into a cold sweat. 'Braden!' she hissed, more loudly this time.

'What's wrong?' He was immediately alert.

'I can hear something.'

He sat up and they both held their breath, listening, and Charley heard again the soft noise of the animal on the other side of the canvas. Then, to her relief, he seemed to be moving away towards the river.

Braden got out of his bag, carefully unzipped the
flap of the tent and went outside, taking his gun with
him. Charley had noticed that he always carried a
gun, though he had never had cause to use it, and
she hoped he wouldn't now. She hoped whatever it
was had gone.

She poked her head out and watched as he woke
the two Indians, and after a few whispered words the
three of them crept off into the darkness.

Charley could see nothing but the dark silhouette
of trees and bushes against the tropical night sky, and
could hear no sound now except the distant roar of
the river. She began to wonder whether she had
imagined the whole thing.

When Braden came back, he announced casually
that it had been a puma. 'But there was no need for
you to worry. He wouldn't have attacked.' He zipped
up the tent and looked at her and Charley could not
keep her limbs still. 'You're cold?' he frowned.

Charley's shirt was pulled over her shoulders and
that was all she had on. But it wasn't cold that was
making her shake. 'I'm scared,' she admitted, and
threw caution to the winds. 'Please hold me,
Braden.'

For a second she thought he was going to mock her
weakness. There was an expression in his eyes that
she could not quite fathom. But then he pulled her to
him, and Charley's fears fled as she felt the strength
of his arms around her and the warmth of his hard-
muscled body. For a while there was nothing sexual
in the embrace, he was offering her the comfort and
reassurance she needed and it was no more than that.

But as the minutes ticked away Charley began to
feel a resurgence of the emotions he had aroused
beneath the waterfall—with a subtle difference. The

water had acted as a lubricant, oiling their skins so that they slid against each other; now she could feel his hair-roughened skin against her soft breasts, and because she was conscious of her nakedness, and because she was afraid that by some movement, or some tiny sound, she might give herself away, she worked her hands up between them and tried to push herself free. 'Thank you,' she said softly. 'I'm all right now.'

'Are you sure?' His dark eyes looked into hers and he made no attempt to let her go.

No, she wasn't sure, but she must free herself before she did something stupid. It was impossible not to be affected by him. 'I want to go back to bed,' she said.

'There doesn't seem much point. It's almost dawn.'

So what was he suggesting they do for the next hour? Spend the time in each other's arms? Charley pushed against him yet again, and felt the steady beat of his heart beneath her palm. It was certainly nowhere near as erratic as her own. How foolish she was to let him affect her like this.

His hands slid up and down her spine—her shirt had long since fallen to the floor—caressing her skin, feeling the shape of her, and Charley felt an insane urge to press herself close, but knew that she mustn't, that it was insanity, that it would lead to something she would later regret. 'I'd still like to rest,' she said, more strongly this time.

'You find the pace too punishing?' he taunted cruelly.

Charley's eyes flashed, as he must have known they would. 'Not in the least.'

'Then why do you want to go back to bed?'

'What else is there to do?' she asked sharply.

'We could sit and watch day break.'

'You sit and watch it,' she snapped, her very awareness of him making her edgy. 'I'll try and get another hour's sleep.' And finally she managed to free herself.

She snuggled down inside her bag and closed her eyes. She heard Braden move and then there was silence. He had not got dressed, so what was he doing? Watching her again? It was a disturbing thought, and Charley could not disregard the inner core of sensation that burned inside her. She clenched her fists and willed herself to fall asleep, but it was impossible. She was wide awake and would remain so until it was time to get up.

But gradually, as all remained silent, some of the tension eased out of her, and by determinedly thinking about her father Charley was able to push thoughts of Braden out of her head.

She really did hope that the Indians on the other side of the range would be able to help them. They had found no evidence so far that they were on the right track, none at all. They were hacking their own way through the jungle and they could be miles off course. The more she thought about it, the more despondent she became. Had she been wise to put all her trust in Braden? Left to herself, she would have taken an entirely different route.

She tossed restlessly and Braden suddenly spoke. 'What are you thinking?'

'About my father.' She twisted her head to look at him. He was sitting cross-legged on top of his sleeping-bag, and as she had rightly guessed he was deliberately watching her.

There was a sudden twist to his lips as she spoke

and Charley wondered whether she had disappointed him. Perhaps he had expected her to say that he was the subject of her thoughts.

'It shouldn't be long now before we have some news of him.'

'*If* he came this way.' Her tone was heavy with sarcasm.

Braden's brows drew together in a frown. 'You still think I'm wrong?'

Charley wriggled into a more comfortable position, making sure the sleeping-bag kept her decently covered. 'I wouldn't dare question your reasoning, but I'd feel better if we'd come across some signs. I know what you said about there being several routes he could have taken, but even so——'

'You don't want to think that I am right?' he cut in coolly.

Charley closed her eyes for a second. 'Of course I want you to be right. I should certainly hate to think that we'd travelled all this way for nothing. But if only we could find some clues, some indication, no matter how trivial, that he had passed this way.'

'Trust in me,' he said, and Charley was reminded of the snake in Rudyard Kipling's *The Jungle Book*. It didn't mean a thing.

'When do you think we'll reach the Indians' camp?'

He looked at her long and hard. 'If I was travelling alone, I'd say late this evening.'

Charley sat up, crossing her arms righteously over herself. 'You can't say that I'm holding you back.'

Their eyes met and held, and it was a long time before he spoke. Then he said, 'Can't I?'

She gasped her disbelief. She had almost killed herself keeping up. Surely even he could not have gone any faster?

He stood up and tugged on his trousers. 'Perhaps if we make an early start and you pull your weight, we might get there today, after all.'

'If we don't, it won't be my fault,' she snapped, and she got up too and began throwing on her clothes. How dared he insinuate that she was hindering them?

She found a mountain spring and washed herself while Jorge cooked the breakfast and Braden and Coyaso loaded the mule. As soon as they had eaten they set off, and Charley discovered that Braden really had been speaking the truth. The pace he set now was nothing short of torture.

For the first hour or so she managed to keep up, but after that Charley found herself going slower and slower. Her mouth was parched, but the flask was on the mule who was up front with the Indians. There was not even a spring where she she could slake her thirst. But Charley refused to suffer the indignity of calling out to them to stop.

By sheer will-power she kept going, but, as another hour passed and the sweat continued to pour out of her, Charley's mouth became so dry that it hurt to breathe.

When occasionally Braden or one of Indians looked back she fixed a brave smile on her face and somehow kept staggering on. But, when the men eventually stopped and Braden turned towards her, Charley could keep up the act no longer and fell in an ignominious heap to the floor.

The next thing she knew, her lips were being moistened and she was lying with her head in the crook of his arm. She struggled to sit up and took the flask, eagerly drinking the beautiful water.

'That was a hell of a stupid thing to do.' Braden's

eyes were hard as he looked at her. 'Have you no more sense than to let yourself get into that state?'

'Why didn't you think to offer me a drink?' she snapped. 'You'd got the water.' Was that all the sympathy she was going to get?

'Oh, I'm sorry,' he said with mock concern, 'I didn't realise I had to mollycoddle you.' Then his lips curled with derision. 'Don't ever let yourself get dehydrated again.'

'If you hadn't been so far in front I could have——' Charley broke off abruptly.

'You could have caught us up? Why didn't you? Were we going too fast?' His eyes narrowed speculatively. 'If we're to reach the Indian camp by nightfall then we can't afford to go any slower. On the other hand, we could settle for reaching them tomorrow. You're the one who's so eager. What's it to be? Kill yourself in the process, or be sensible and take it a little easier?'

Charley closed her eyes, breathing deeply and angrily. She hated having to admit that it was too much, but it was senseless punishing herself when another day would make no difference. 'I can't keep up that pace,' she admitted, finally looking at him.

'A fact that I've known all along,' he said tersely. 'The reason I would have preferred to go alone.'

'Is it the length of time it will take that's bothering you, Mr Quest? Have you set yourself a time limit? Have you got other commitments? If you're going to lose money, then rest assured that——'

'I told you I don't want payment,' he snarled.

'But you just don't like the idea of a woman tagging along? I'm so sorry, but you knew what it would be like before you accepted. I feel better now, shall we go?'

His nostrils dilated angrily. 'I don't need a martyr, either. Sit and rest a while, sip the water, but not too much at once. We'll scout on ahead and then come back for you. We won't be long, a half-hour at the most. That should give you enough time to regain your strength.'

After conferring with Jorge and Coyaso, they all three disappeared into the undergrowth. Charley took another drink of water and, leaning back against the bole of a tree, closed her eyes. She did not mean to go to sleep but she must have done so because she was woken by the sound of a shot, and when she looked up Braden was pointing his gun at her.

Panic flared in her eyes and fear raced through her. She struggled to sit up. Had he gone mad? What was he doing? Oh, lord, what was going on? Perhaps she was hallucinating? This wasn't real, it couldn't be.

'Don't move!' he barked, and Coyaso neatly flicked away with a stick the snake that was lying half across her legs. It was quite dead. Braden's aim had been true. But he could have shot her! Another few inches and—Charley went quite cold at the thought.

She tried to speak, but only managed a croak. 'What happened?' And this time it wasn't because of thirst.

'You moved in your sleep and disturbed a snake while he was harmlessly gliding by. He naturally wanted to defend himself and——'

'He was about to bite me?' she gasped incredulously.

Braden nodded. 'We came back in the nick of time.'

'What if you'd missed him? Or worse still, what if you'd shot me?' Her blue eyes were saucer-wide in her pale face.

'That was a risk I had to take,' he shrugged.

He sounded so casual that Charley could have screamed, and suddenly she began to shake uncontrollably. She had been close to death without even knowing it.

Braden put his gun away. 'For Pete's sake, pull your-self together. Surely this isn't the first time you've faced danger.'

'Of course not,' she snapped, and his harsh words were far more effective than if he had offered sympathy. Not that he could have known this. He was an unfeeling brute and at this moment she hated him.

'Then get up and let's move. Much more of this and we'll be lucky to make that Indian camp by the end of the week.'

Charley glared as she struggled to her feet, and her limbs felt like jelly. She rested one hand for a moment against the tree, taking several deep steady breaths. Jorge and Coyaso were watching her anxiously. Braden was checking the mule's load.

'OK, I'm ready,' she said, and once again they set off. This time their pace was much slower and she was able to keep up, and when they stopped for lunch Charley was feeling almost her normal self.

By nightfall they had one more ridge to climb. 'We should have news of your father by lunch time tomorrow,' Braden announced with satisfaction after they had finished their meal.

'I've not held you up too much, after all?' she enquired archly.

He eyed her for a moment, then a tiny grudging smile appeared at the corner of his mouth. 'You've done well—for a woman.'

Praise indeed—coming from him. 'I told you I was good, but you wouldn't believe me,' she replied with a flash of her eyes. 'Goodnight, Braden, I'm going to turn in. Goodnight Jorge, Coyaso.'

'Me, too,' Braden said, much to her surprise. He usually sat on chatting to the other two for well over an hour after she had gone to bed. He never said what they were talking about and she never asked. But obviously tonight he had nothing to say.

Despite the fact that she ought to be used to Braden seeing her in a state of undress, Charley felt embarrassed stripping in front of him and she shot into her sleeping-bag the second her clothes were off, sitting up and hugging her knees, but making sure she was covered to her chin.

He chuckled. 'What's wrong?' And he proceeded to unbutton his shirt in a leisurely fashion and unzip his trousers. 'Surely you're not still afraid of me looking at you?'

'Of course not,' she said swiftly.

'Then you're afraid I might touch you? Don't you like me touching you, Charley?'

What was all this in aid of? she wondered. Why was he taunting her? 'I don't think this trip is the time or the place to indulge in a casual flirtation,' she replied coolly. 'All that I'm concerned with is finding my father.'

'But you are aware of me—as a man—as a possible lover—and don't deny it,' he added quickly as she began to protest. 'It's as obvious to me as if you were holding up a banner announcing the fact.'

'How the hell do you know what I'm feeling?' she questioned angrily. 'Are you an expert on women?'

His lips twisted wryly. 'I think I'm capable of reading the signs.'

'OK, so what?' she demanded. 'I do find you physically attractive—sometimes. But it doesn't mean that I'm proud of it!'

'What would your response be if I said that I find you attractive, too?'

Charley eyed him in astonishment. 'I wouldn't

'believe you. You've made it perfectly clear what you think of me.'

His brows rose. 'I have?'

'Yes, you have.'

'So what is my opinion of you?' He finished undressing and sat down on his sleeping-bag, facing her. The lamp cast a shadow across his face and it was difficult to read his true expression.

'You think I'm weak. You think I'm incapable. You think it was madness bringing me with you.'

'I'm not talking about your prowess as an adventurer,' he said softly. 'I'm talking about you as a person, a female, a very feminine woman. Take the braids out of your hair, Charley. Let me see it loose about your shoulders. It's the way I like it best.'

Charley felt her heart-beats quicken. 'I don't believe you find me attractive in that way.'

He frowned. 'Why do you say that?'

'You've had every opportunity to—to——' She shook her head, balking at finding the right words.

But Braden had no such reservations. 'Make love to you?'

Charley swallowed hard and nodded, her eyes troubled.

His brows lifted. 'And what's happened every time I kiss you? I've told you before, I never force myself on anyone.' His tone dropped to a low, sexy growl. 'And I don't intend to force myself on you, Charley.'

He leaned forward and took the bands out of her plaits, and she was powerless to stop him. Then he ran his fingers through her hair, lifting it, setting it free, letting it fall in thick, heavy waves. And gently he eased the sleeping-bag down to her waist and arranged her hair over her nakedness, almost but not quite covering her breasts.

Then he sat back and looked at her, and Charley felt herself tingling from head to toe. She touched her tongue to her lips and her breathing became shallow. She wondered what he was going to do next.

'You're quite beautiful,' he said. And he was the most sexy man she had ever met. 'You don't look like the girl who's grimly determined to keep up at whatever cost. Or the one who'd like to kill me because I'm setting too hard a pace.'

Charley's eyes widened. He always seemed oblivious of her. Apparently she had misjudged him. And quite definitely she wasn't feeling the same now. He was right on that score. She felt totally defenceless, her body responding to his masculinity of its own volition.

He held out a hand, palm uppermost. 'Come here.'

After only the slightest hesitation Charley put her hand into his and on her knees moved over to him. Their eyes met and held, and the sensations in her body were increasing by the second. She wished he would kiss her or hold her or do something instead of just looking at her.

When he touched her face with his fingertips, exploring slowly and seductively each curve and hollow, the shape of her nose, the softness of her mouth, she closed her eyes, savouring each movement, and it felt as though he were branding her. Her head sank back lower and lower on her shoulders, and when he moistened a finger in his own mouth and ran it across her lips she moaned in an agony of pleasure. This was sheer mental torture.

'Charley.' He lifted her chin and made her look at him. 'Kiss me.' A tiny sound of protest escaped her lips. 'I know you want to.'

And he was going to take no risk of her rejecting him. He wanted *her* to make the running. 'I can't,' she whispered.

'Why not?'

'It's not what I want.'

'I think it is.'

And he was right. She wanted to kiss him very much, but where would it lead? Why submit to temptation when it meant nothing, not to him, anyway? So far as her own feelings were concerned, she was not so sure. He was growing on her. There were times when she hated him passionately, others when she could not ignore the emotions he aroused. And at this precise moment those feelings were very strong indeed.

'I'm waiting.' He cupped her face and looked at her long and hard, then he slid his fingers through the thickness of her hair and, holding her head, urged her slowly but firmly towards him, stopping just short of their lips meeting. Charley had no choice.

She closed her eyes and pressed her mouth to his, lightly at first, but soon deepening to hunger as the touch of him sent frissons of awareness through her limbs. She slid her arms around him and his naked chest brushed against her breasts. A tremor ran through her.

Charley kissed him then as he had her. She kissed his mouth, his eyes, his cheeks, his ears, she discovered every angle and every plane, and by the time she came back to his mouth her breathing had quickened and she was not quite sure what she was doing.

Braden was the submissive partner no longer, now it was his turn to pour the heat of his passion into her. With a groan he crushed her to him, his tongue urgently seeking the soft moistness of her mouth. Charley knew that all sorts of tiny sounds were escaping her throat, but she could not help herself. She had never felt so completely wanton before. All else was forgotten in the hat of the moment.

When his hand moulded her aching breast, when his thumb grazed her nipple into sensitive hardness, yet more shivers of sensation shot through her. No man had ever touched her so intimately. In her formative teenage years boys had tried to fondle her, but nothing had prepared her for the ecstasy of Braden's touch.

And when his mouth sought the hollow of her throat, moving slowly and searingly downwards, and when his tongue rasping over her pert nipple set every nerve-end on fire, Charley felt completely abandoned.

He paid the same attention to her other breast, and when he looked at her again his mouth was moist and dark and she touched it wonderingly with the tips of her fingers. 'That was beautiful,' she whispered. She didn't want him to stop. She wanted him to go on and on. He was spiralling her somewhere into a seventh heaven.

'For me, too.' There was a huskiness in his tone which suggested a need to have more of her also, to prolong their lovemaking. Perhaps even to spend the whole night together. 'But you'd best go to bed now, or goodness knows what I might do next. You're truly amazing.'

'I am?' A tiny frown creased her brow.

'For a girl who professes to think and act like a man, for a girl who's constantly tried to keep me at a distance, yes, you are.'

'I couldn't help myself,' she said with faint embarrassment.

'And if you don't move away from me I won't be able to help myself,' he threatened. Even as he spoke his fingers touched and stroked her breasts, and Charley ached with a longing to be completely possessed by him. But it would be wrong. Once this trip was over, once they found out what had happened to her father, she would never see him again. He wanted her now, yes, but that was because he was a man and she was a woman and it was inevitable. Under other circumstances he would not have looked at her twice.

It was with reluctance, though, that she finally pulled away from him and crawled back into her sleeping-bag. Braden slid into his and put out the lamp, but Charley knew she would have difficulty in sleeping. Her whole body tingled from top to toe, and she thought she was falling in love.

CHAPTER FIVE

WHEN they set off the next morning there was a lift to Charley's step, and it wasn't because of what had happened last night, devastating though that had been. Today they should have some news about her father. This was what the whole trip was about. She must never lose sight of it for one second.

As usual Braden strode on ahead with Jorge and Coyaso, the mule plodding behind, and Charley bringing up the rear. And for once she did not mind. When she awoke Braden had already left the tent and she had lain for several minutes remembering his kisses. Her whole body had warmed at the thought of his touching her, and now she was able to watch him without his being aware of it.

He was the most aggressively masculine man she had ever met. He was several inches taller than the Indian boys, with broad shoulders and powerful arms and legs. He was tough and vital, as well as being overpoweringly sexy. He never seemed to tire. He looked as though he could go on all day without a rest.

But it was foolish of her to fall in love with him, and she must do her best to make sure that he never knew. Perhaps it wasn't even love that she felt. Perhaps it was purely physical attraction. In which case she would cope much better knowing that in the end they could part and she would feel no sorrow.

Her legs ached intolerably by the time they topped the last rise, and she was glad when Braden called a halt. They had travelled much further then usual without a rest, but somehow the knowlege that they were so near to hearing about her father had given her the strength to carry on.

She dropped to the grass and was shocked when Braden told her curtly to get up and collect sticks for the fire. 'I know it's early,' he said, 'but we may as well have lunch now, then we can keep going until we reach the Indian encampment.'

It was normally Jorge and Coyaso who searched for wood, and she glared at Braden angrily. This wasn't the first time he had been like this after kissing her. It was as though he regretted his moment of weakness and needed to take it out on her. OK, so let him. She wouldn't argue. But he need not think she would let him kiss her again. If this was going to be her payment then he could keep his kisses to himself.

Once replete, they resumed their journey, and when they were within earshot of where Braden presumed the camp to be Coyaso gave a long, loud yodel, which Charley knew was the normal practice when approaching Indians. It was not wise to turn up unannounced in case they were unfriendly.

By the time they reached the bottom of the hill their way was barred by three men standing across the track. They were dressed in knee-length cloaks, their hair was tied back with plain headbands and they looked anything but friendly.

Charley's first thought was that these people might have harmed her father, and a shiver of fear chilled her spine. She glanced at Braden and he touched a hand to her shoulder. 'Wait here,' he said. 'I'll go and talk to them.'

She watched anxiously as he approached the group of Indians and spoke to them for a long time without appearing to make progress. Then he beckoned to Jorge and Coyaso.

After what seemed like hours of talking, although it could only have been minutes, Braden came back to her. 'It's all right, they'll let us stay the night.'

'But my father, what did they say about my father?' asked Charley impatiently, her forehead creased into a deep, puzzled frown. Surely he hadn't spent the whole time asking whether they could pitch their tent?

'I haven't asked them about him yet,' he answered levelly.

Charley could not believe it. 'Then what took you so long?' she gasped.

The glance he gave her was one a parent levelled at a child who was asking stupid questions. 'You, above anyone else, should know that not all Indians are friendly. I had the devil's own job persuading them that we meant no harm.'

'We don't have to stay here, we just want to know what's happened to my father.'

'And they will tell us in their own good time. I sensed a need to win their confidence before we started asking questions.'

There was nothing else Charley could say. She shrugged her shoulders and began walking towards the first group of thatched huts.

As they pitched their tent in an open space they were surrounded by children who watched them, open-mouthed, and with less fear than the adults who either glanced at them from a discreet distance or went about their work as though they did not exist.

Braden offered the children sweets which they took shyly but delightedly. 'Some of them have probably never seen a white man,' explained Braden.

'How about my father?' she asked at once. 'They would have seen him.'

'Perhaps,' he said with some impatience. 'We'll have to wait and see.'

Charley thought he was being unnecessarily cautious and knew that if she could speak Quechua, or whatever language it was that these Indians spoke, she would ask them outright if they had seen her parent. He was wasting time. If they knew, they could be off first thing in the morning. Now they would have to wait until Braden thought it appropriate to pop the question.

She could not sleep that night. Not through fear of the Indians, but through anxiety. They were so near and yet so far to finding out whether Spencer had passed this way, whether in fact he was hidden in their midst, although somehow she doubted that. She would have sensed his presence, surely.

These weren't the people who Braden thought had persuaded her father to stay with them. No, that was some other group, and their methods of persuasion frightened her. What if he were being kept against his will? What chance would the four of them have against a whole village of maybe over a hundred Indians? What if they found her father and then couldn't persuade the Indians to let him come home? What if her father himself did not want to return? Charley did not think she could bear that.

'For pity's sake, go to sleep.'

Braden's harsh voice reached her as she changed position for the hundredth time. 'I can't,' she snapped. Did he think she would be tossing and turning like this if she could?

'Then at least lie still and let me get some sleep.'

For a few resentful minutes Charley managed to do as he asked but then she forgot his admonition and thrashed about once more. The next second Braden uttered an oath and she heard him scrambling out of bed, but nothing prepared her for him unzipping her sleeping-bag and sliding in beside her.

'Braden!' she choked. 'What the devil do you think you're doing? Get out!'

He wrapped one leg over hers and his arm lay heavy about her waist. 'Making sure you don't move again,' he growled, his breath warm on her cheek.

He was also making sure that she did not get any sleep, thought Charley. Incensed as she was, she could not ignore the flutter of awareness his naked body created, and it crossed her mind to wonder whether he would have slept in the nude if he had been alone. It had probably been a deliberate attempt on his part right from the beginning to make her sexually aware of him—and it had succeeded far beyond anything he could have imagined.

Keeping still now was torture. Every inch of her body was sensitised, every breath she took she could smell the musky odour of him, and she was more awake now than when she'd come to bed.

But clearly Braden felt no such awareness. His breathing deepened, his limbs grew heavy, and finally he slept, and it angered Charley that he could sleep with her in his arms, that having her so close meant nothing.

On the other hand, had he tried to make love she would have fought him every inch of the way. It was just as well that he had gone to sleep, even if it didn't do much for her ego. She shifted carefully into a more comfortable position, and with her head resting on his shoulder she, too, slept.

When she awoke Charley had the bag to herself
and Braden was pulling on his trousers. But the
second she opened her eyes he looked down at her.
'Good morning,' he smiled.

'Good morning,' she answered hesitantly. There
was an expression on his face she could not quite
fathom. A sort of secret pleasure. Her body grew
warm. Had something happened during the night
that she remembered nothing about? He looked like a
man well satisfied with himself. She recalled her
dream.

In it, she and Braden were alone in the jungle. He
was wearing a white tuxedo and she a long white
evening dress that glittered with pearls and sequins.
They both held machetes and calmly hacked their
way through the undergrowth, neither finding it
incongruous that they were dressed in such a
manner. They seemed to be searching for somewhere
and finally found an idyllic glade where they calmly
undressed and lay down in each other's arms.

The grass was soft beneath them and his hands
explored every intimate place of her body, and she in
her turn touched him. They did not actually make
love. They seemed not to need that, just this hunger
to touch and feel, to explore one another's bodies, to
know exactly what the other felt like.

He had kissed her all over and a shudder ran
through Charley as she remembered how her own
lips had trailed over the tanned, silken firmness of his
body.

'What are you thinking?'

Charley brought herself back to the present with a
start, her blue eyes over-bright as she looked up at
him. 'I had a dream, it's nothing, just——' She tailed
off uncertainly.

'Care to tell me about it?' He squatted down and sub-
jected her to a gaze so intense that every nerve in her
body screamed. She wondered how much of her dream
had been in the mind, and how much actual fact. He
had touched her, she felt sure. It was there in his eyes,
Or was it? Charley wished she could be certain.

'No, I wouldn't,' she said. 'It was just a crazy mixed-
up dream.'

'Was I in it?'

She nodded.

His mouth quirked at the corners and he shot up
again and began pulling on his shirt. 'Tell me, what was
I doing that was so crazy? I'm not sure I like the sound
of that.'

'Nothing,' she lied, feeling the colour mount her
cheeks.

'I was doing—nothing? Come on, Charley, the look
on your face tells me I was doing something that
threatened your sanity. Was it a——'

Charley could stand his mockery no longer. She put
her hands over her ears and said harshly, 'Shut up! Just
shut up, will you? I don't want to talk about it.'

'Because you think it might not have been a dream?'

She turned her head angrily away from him.

His laughter taunted her. 'What wouldn't I give to
see into your mind right now? Poor Charley. A dream
or not a dream, that is the question. I'm sure our
immortal bard will forgive me for misquoting his
words.' And with one more chuckle he unzipped the
tent and disappeared.

Charley quickly got up and pulled on her clothes,
fuming, hating him, yet fully aware of the power he
wielded over her. She was suddenly not her own
woman, her body and mind were behaving in an alien
manner, and she did not like it. She had always

enjoyed her independence, she had enjoyed being an equal to her father and Alan, and now all that was suddenly over. She was no equal to Braden, she never would be. And the more time they spent together, the more feminine she felt. It was becoming a very difficult situation.

They spent the whole day talking to the Indians—at least, Braden did. Charley could only sit and listen and wait for his interpretation. She gave a couple of blouses to the Indian women and they became very friendly, but it was no help when she could not understand a word they said.

It was early evening before Braden told her that several weeks ago her father had also stayed at this camp.

'So we really are on his track?' she asked excitedly, her heart suddenly racing. 'Which way did he go?'

A rueful grimace creased Braden's face. 'There are conflicting opinions about that. It's a matter of deciding which one we think is most likely.' He reached out his map and spread it on the ground. Charley knelt beside him. Her father's proposed destination was circled in red, and so far as she could see the most obvious route would be directly north-east.

'He'd have gone this way,' she said, looking into Braden's face. His eyes glittered like silver in the fading daylight, and Charley felt herself momentarily losing herself in their depths.

'The most direct route is not always the easiest,' he told her.

'I realise that,' she replied. He really had the most beautiful eyes she had ever seen. Just one look from them was like a caress. It was an effort to turn away and concentrate on the map.

'Some of the Indians believe he went this way.'
Braden moved his finger in a winding arc. 'And I'm
inclined to believe them.'

'But it will take us weeks as against days,' she
protested, 'and if my father has actually reached the
lost city then we would be wasting time.'

'And if he hasn't, if he's somewhere *en route*, we
would miss him.'

'You really think he would have gone the long way
round?' she asked doubtfully. Knowing her father as
she did, she felt sure he would have taken the short-
est path. He always did. On the other hand, he was
getting no younger, and, if this other track was
easier, then just possibly he might have taken it.
Time was of no importance.

Again Charley berated herself for not having
shown more interest. She had believed Rupert
Billings' story to be a whole load of hogwash, and
now regretted not discussing it in more detail with
her father.

'If I were going, that's what I would do,' he said,
'and on the one occasion that I met your father we
did discover that we had remarkably similar ideas.'

He moved fractionally and his thigh brushed hers,
and a surge of pure pleasure flooded through
Charley. 'In that case,' she said, swallowing hard,
'that's the way we'll go.' And she pushed herself up.

She felt sure he had deliberately moved closer. He
knew exactly what he was doing. It was his way of
making this mission more pleasurable. He hadn't
wanted her, but since she was here he intended
making the most of his opportunities. It was just a
fun-game to him. She was the prey and he the
predator, and he was toying with her like a cat does
with a mouse.

Cursing herself for responding so obviously, Charley made a silent vow that in future she would keep him at arm's length. She would make it clear that she was not interested in him in a sexual way. They were one of a team looking for her father and she would be obliged if he would treat her as such. The trouble was, they were a man and a woman with a man's and a woman's sexual appetites.

Which would be all right if he loved her. It would help make this search less traumatic. She would have the excitement of a love affair to cushion the anxiety she felt over her father's disappearance. But sex for the sake of sex was not in her line of thinking. It never had been. When she committed herself to a man it would be because she truly loved him and wanted to marry him. And, even though at this moment she thought she could be in love with Braden, he certainly had no such feelings for her, so it was best they kept their distance.

'We'll head off at dawn,' he told her, standing too. 'So if I were you I'd get an early night.'

Charley looked at him with a a faint frown, feeling pretty sure that he meant to join her in the tent, and that the suggested early night was no more than an excuse.

'I'll try not to wake you when I turn in,' he said, and his smile told her that he knew exactly what she was thinking. 'I have some haggling to do for supplies. Goodnight.' And he walked away.

Charley decided that she would never understand him, not in a thousand years. Just when she had begun to think that he intended to take advantage of her, he was behaving like a gentleman.

It was with mixed feelings that she went to bed, and because she had done nothing all day she wasn't tired. She stretched out and looked up at the canvas ceiling of the tent and thought about Braden. How could she not think about him? Naturally her father filled her thoughts to a very large extent, but Braden was here in the flesh and there was no way she could ignore him.

He excited her so much it was ridiculous, and how could she keep it from him? He was too perceptive by far. Just now when they had been poring over the map he had known the reason she had jumped up so quickly. His thigh against hers had been an igniting of the flesh, and had she remained in that position Charley knew she would have given in to temptation.

She turned on her side but was still awake when Braden came into the tent. He did not speak, though, and she decided it was best to let him think her asleep.

Listening to the sound of him undressing was like actually watching him. She could visualise his broad, tanned chest, his hard, flat stomach and narrow hips. The whipcord quality of his arms, his powerfully muscled legs. She heard the rasp of nylon against his skin as he slid into his sleeping-bag. And then there was silence.

Charley listened to the sound of his breathing, waiting for it to deepen. When he was asleep she knew she would sleep, too. Only then would she feel safe, but whether it was from him or herself she could not be sure.

When his voice broke the silence it startled her. 'Not asleep yet, Charley?'

She did not answer.

'Could it be that you were waiting for me?'

The conceit of the man! She jerked her head round to look at him, but it was too dark to see more than his outline. 'Why would I do that?'

'Because I think you're beginning to enjoy the moments we spend together.'

'You're not coming in my bed again,' she snapped.

'I wouldn't dream of it, it's far too uncomfortable. But if we zipped our sleeping-bags together we'd have room to——'

'Go to hell!' she cried. 'Do you really think that because I once forgot myself you can maul me whenever it takes your fancy?'

'Maul you?' he snapped. 'Is that what it felt like? Is that really what you think I was doing?' He paused, but Charley could hear his angry breathing. Then he went on, 'I'm sorry, Charley.' His tone was heavy with sarcasm. 'I'm really very sorry. Remind me never to touch you again.'

He hunched away from her and was silent, and Charley knew she ought to apologise, but if she did they would end up in each other's arms, and she did not want that. It was best to let him go on thinking this way.

Eventually she slept, but it seemed like only minutes before Braden was shaking her and telling her to get up.

Hard day followed hard day. Braden was relentless in his pursuit of their goal. There were no more intimacies between them and he granted her no favours. In fact, he handed her a machete and made her do her share of the work.

Her hands developed blisters and grew calluses, but she never once complained. Her arms and shoulders ached and her muscles protested, but she soldiered on. This was what she had asked for and it would be fatal to complain. In fact, she quite enjoyed it. If only he would be that little bit easier, not pushing her to breaking-point all the time. If only he would consider her occasionally instead of treating her with indifference. He actually seemed friendlier towards Jorge and Coyaso then he did towards her.

The only good part about it all was that at night she fell into an immediate exhausted sleep. Braden and even her father were forgotten. She couldn't have managed a physical affair had she wanted one.

Her conversations with Braden centred almost entirely on the Inca culture. They both avoided personal topics, and not by so much as the bat of an eyelid did he suggest that he was in any way attracted to her. He ignored her totally when they went to bed, and contrarily Charley found herself hungering for him. A gentle touch, a light kiss, a few soft words, would have been enough. Instead of which there was nothing. Absolutely nothing.

In the end his treatment of her made her bad-tempered, and when one day he castigated her for not hacking a path quickly enough she turned on him angrily. 'I've had enough.' She threw her machete to the ground. 'When are you going to realise that I'm not built the same as you men? That I can't lift and hammer and chop as easily and as quickly as you?'

'I already know it,' he said. 'It was you who wanted to be treated as an equal. Backing out, are you?'

His bland smile infuriated Charley even more, and her nostrils flared as she faced him, her blue eyes flashed, her fingers curled into tight fists. 'No, I am not backing out. I actually think that I am doing all right, and if you were man enough to admit it you'd say so, too. What the hell is it with you that you're on my back all the time?' She was not worried about the Indians listening because they did not understand English, although they were watching them with an openly curious expression. 'Is it because you're frustrated? Is it because I refuse to have sex with you? Is that what it is? My God, if that's all you can think about, then I pity you.'

His eyes grew cold and his mouth hardened. 'It's obvious that's what's on *your* mind. Perhaps we ought to satiate our appetites right here and now.' He moved menacingly towards her. 'Perhaps we ought to get rid of that energy you're using in the wrong direction.'

'Keep away from me,' she cried.

'Why should I?' There was an ugly leer on his face now and his hands shot out to grip her upper arms. 'Why should I? You're behaving like a child, Charley. If you can't accept criticism, then you should never have come in the first place.'

She eyed him hotly. 'If criticism is justified then I would be the first to accept it, but just because I'm not as strong as you three I resent most strongly being told to work harder. I've worked my guts out this last week or so without one single word of complaint. Look at my hands, look at them! Are those the hands of a girl who's not pulling her weight?'

He frowned down at her cracked and callused hands. 'I had no idea.'

'No, you wouldn't have, would you? You were so intent on punishing me that you never spared a thought for my well-being. So long as I was coping, that was all you cared about.'

'I did what I had to do,' he crisped. 'You can't deny that we've made better progress.'

'No, I don't, and I'm quite willing to carry on as we're doing, but I will not accept unfair censure.'

He picked up her knife and tucked it into the mule's pack. 'Let's get going.'

His voice was tight, but there was no apology. She had expected none. Neither had she expected that he would take the machete off her. She wanted to work. Besides, if she stopped now it would make her hands soft, and when Braden decided to make her work alongside them again it would be all the harder.

But she did not voice her thoughts. She would wait until morning and then she would carry on as she had these last days, regardless of what Braden said.

The next day, though, he raised no objection to her using the knife, and Charley's hope for a verbal battle fell flat. In fact, he seemed to expect it of her, and if he had felt any remorse yesterday he was certainly feeling none today.

For several hours they walked. It was not all hard going, they came across some wide, flat, open spaces where it was hardly overgrown at all, and when Braden questioned the Indians they said that it was part of an old Inca site.

Immediately out came Braden's camera and various photographs were taken. He pointed out a semicircle of stones that were covered with grass and small plants and not immediately visible. 'Obviously a kind of a court,' he said, and he made a reference on his map so that he could enquire into it at a later date.

It began to irk her that he only spoke when there was something of interest to discuss. He never asked her how she was feeling or coping. He never asked whether she would like to rest. He never talked to her about her home life or her hobbies, or even very much about her father. Apart from the incident yesterday when she thought she had seen some compassion, that was all the personal interest he had shown in her. And today was no different from any other day.

After lunch Coyaso came to a sudden halt and began pointing and talking quickly and excitedly.

'What is it?' she asked Braden eagerly. There was nothing in front of them except a valley with a river running along the bottom, and beyond that another range of seemingly endless mountains. She could see no sign of habitation.

'If we follow the river to the foot of those hills,' he pointed a finger in the same direction that the Indian had indicated, 'then cross it where it meets another great river, then follow the line of that hill—in the next valley are Indians whose *Sinchi Kooto* is a Blue Eyes.'

Their chief was a white man! Charley looked at Braden wide-eyed. 'You don't think that——'

'No, it wouldn't be your father,' he said at once. 'It's been a long time since Coyaso was last there.'

'But maybe he's talking about the man you said had died?'

'I don't think so,' he frowned. 'These aren't the Indians that I was thinking of.'

'But there is a chance that my father's there?'

'There's every chance, of course,' he said at once, 'and we must explore each possibility.'

Charley's adrenalin began to flow. 'How long do you think it will take us to get there?'

He lifted his broad shoulders. 'A couple of days.'

'Can't we do it any quicker?'

'I think we're making the best time we can.'

'If I work harder?'

For a brief second his face softened. 'I think you're already overdoing it.'

Her eyes met his. 'No, I'm not.' But she was surprised he had said such a thing.

'No? Let me look at your hands.' He took them and

studied the hard skin. 'Not the hands of a lady.'

'I've never said I was one. I enjoy what I do.'

'You've also lost weight.'

He had noticed that, too? He surprised her. 'I always do when I'm on one of these expeditions.'

'It's not good for you.'

'I don't feel ill.'

'Maybe not now, but we're not there yet and we still have the journey back. I think you should leave the bulk of the hard work to me and Jorge and Coyaso.'

'I want no favours.'

'I'm not granting you any. I'm thinking of your health. I don't want an invalid on my hands.'

And he spoke the truth. She had worked harder than at any other time in her life. Her father would never have let her do so much manual work. And they were so far away from civilisation that it would be an impossibility to get her back quickly if she did fall ill. But she had no intention of giving him the opportunity to say again that she was not pulling her weight. 'I can cope,' she said quietly.

'And I'm telling you to take things easier.'

There was a hard note in his voice now and she looked at him coolly. 'Is that an order?'

'Yes, it is,' he clipped.

'Very well—sir,' she added smartly, and something impish inside her almost made her salute him, but she did not think he would appreciate that. In fact, he was already frowning. But he said no more and they continued their journey.

Once Charley had nothing more to do than follow the men and the mule, whom she had named Stalwart because he was so steadfast and strong, she had more time to look about her. The valley was brilliantly green and one nearby summit was built entirely of huge overlapping slabs of rock all slanting in the same direction. And the sky was a cloudless dark blue such as it never was in England.

Their tracks took them along the edges of the forest-like jungle with a waterfall leaping and sparkling through the tracery of branches. Parrots and other brilliantly coloured birds flitted in and out. Finally they came to a high plateau covered in lush green grass. Stalwart was in his element, and they decided to make camp there for the night.

Charley cooked their meal, fresh fish caught by Jorge, and boiled maize, followed by bananas and mangoes that they had picked on their travels, and after that there was nothing to do but go to bed.

She was excited now that they were nearing an Indian camp where possibly she would find her father, or at the very least she would be able to speak to the white man there, the Blue Eyes as the Quechua Indians called all white men. Who was he? What could he tell them? Braden was the only person she had spoken to in weeks, apart from sign language with Jorge and Coyaso. It would be so good to talk to someone else.

Braden joined her in the tent while she was still sitting with her hands clasped about her knees.

'You look happier,' he commented as he began to undress.

'I feel we're on the verge of finding something out at last.'

'It isn't because you're not now killing yourself with hard work?'

She glanced at him angrily. 'Are you sorry you said I needn't do any more? Don't throw it at me, Braden, it wasn't my idea. I'm perfectly willing to go on. I always have been. It was you in the first place who

The more
you love romance . . .
the more
you'll love this offer

FREE!

Mail this heart today! (see inside)!

**Join us on a Harlequin Honeymoon
and we'll give you
4 free books
A free bracelet watch
And a free mystery gift**

IT'S A
HARLEQUIN HONEYMOON—
A SWEETHEART
OF A FREE OFFER!
HERE'S WHAT YOU GET:

1. **Four New Harlequin Romance® Novels—FREE!**
   Take a Harlequin Honeymoon with your four exciting
   romances—yours FREE from Harlequin Reader Service®. Each
   of these hot-off-the-press novels brings you the passion and ten-
   derness of today's greatest love stories . . . your free passports to
   bright new worlds of love and foreign adventure.

2. **A Lovely Bracelet Watch—FREE!**
   You'll love your elegant bracelet watch—this classic LCD quartz
   watch is a perfect expression of your style and good taste—and it
   is yours FREE as an added thanks for giving our Reader Service
   a try.

3. **An Exciting Mystery Bonus—FREE!**
   You'll be thrilled with this surprise gift. It is elegant as well as
   practical.

4. **Money-Saving Home Delivery!**
   Join Harlequin Reader Service® and enjoy the convenience of
   previewing eight new books every month delivered right to your
   home. Each book is yours for only $2.24*—26¢ less per book than
   the cover price—plus only 89¢ postage and handling for the en-
   tire shipment! Great savings plus total convenience add up to a
   sweetheart of a deal for you! If you're not completely satisfied,
   you may cancel at any time, for any reason, simply by sending us
   a note or shipping statement marked "cancel" or by returning any
   shipment to us at our cost.

5. **Free Insiders' Newsletter**
   It's *heart to heart*®, the indispensible insiders' look at our most
   popular writers, upcoming books, comments from readers and
   much more!

6. **More Surprise Gifts**
   Because our home subscribers are our most valued readers, when
   you join the Harlequin Reader Service®, we'll be sending you ad-
   ditional free gifts from time to time—as a token of our
   appreciation.

START YOUR HARLEQUIN HONEYMOON TODAY—JUST
COMPLETE, DETACH AND MAIL YOUR FREE-OFFER CARD

Get your fabulous gifts
ABSOLUTELY FREE!

MAIL THIS CARD TODAY.

PLACE
HEART STICKER
HERE

GIVE YOUR HEART
TO HARLEQUIN

YES! Please send me my four Harlequin Romance® novels FREE, along with my free bracelet watch and free mystery gift. I wish to receive all the benefits of the Harlequin Reader Service® as explained on the opposite page.

NAME _____
(PLEASE PRINT)

ADDRESS _____ APT. _____

CITY _____ PROV. _____

POSTAL CODE _____ 318 CIH WAVE (C-H-R-09/89)

OFFER LIMITED TO ONE PER HOUSEHOLD AND NOT VALID TO CURRENT HARLEQUIN ROMANCE® SUBSCRIBERS. ALL ORDERS SUBJECT TO APPROVAL.

HARLEQUIN READER SERVICE® "NO RISK" GUARANTEE

—There's no obligation to buy—and the free books and gifts remain yours to keep.
—You pay the low members-only discount price and receive books before they appear in stores.
—You may end your subscription anytime by sending us a note or shipping statement marked "cancel" or by returning any shipment to us at our cost.

START YOUR
HARLEQUIN HONEYMOON TODAY.
JUST COMPLETE, DETACH AND MAIL YOUR
FREE OFFER CARD.

If offer card is missing, write to: Harlequin Reader Service® P.O. Box 609
Fort Erie, Ontario L2A 5X3

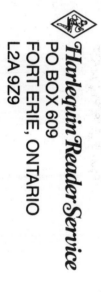

**Business
Reply Mail**

No Postage Stamp
Necessary if Mailed
in Canada

Postage will be paid by

Harlequin Reader Service
PO BOX 609
FORT ERIE, ONTARIO
L2A 9Z9

Canada Post
Postes Canada
125

DETACH AND MAIL TODAY!

seemed to think I wasn't capable. Haven't I proved myself?'

'Oh, yes, you've proved it,' he said drily, 'but what am I supposed to do, congratulate you? Women who do men's work don't impress me. I've never been able to understand what they're trying to prove.'

'In my case,' she said, 'I've always done it for my father. He wanted a mate, a partner, and I tried my hardest to be that for him.'

'And he didn't care that his beautiful daughter dressed and acted like a boy and probably never experienced the magic and excitement of growing into an attractive young lady, of being loved and falling in love?'

'I've had plenty of boyfriends,' she protested. 'I'm not away from home all the time, you know.'

'But never any serious relationships,'

Her chin lifted. 'Who told you that?'

'Your mother.'

'She had no right. What else has she told you about me?'

'Oh, this and that. It's such a pity, Charley. A very great pity.'

He took the band out of her hair and as the black locks fell free he once again arranged it about her shoulders. 'You're a very beautiful young lady. You should be wearing pretty dresses and meeting all the right people, not traipsing through the jungle with hardened explorers like me. Don't you ever yearn for romance? Don't you ever wish a handsome young man would come along and sweep you off your feet?'

'There's plenty of time for that,' she said, hoping he could not hear the sudden pounding of her heart.

'You're twenty-four. Most girls your age are married with families.'

'So what? I'm hardly over the hill.'

'No, but if you carry on like this you soon will be. Your English-rose complexion will suffer and look more like tanned leather.'

'And I think you have an infernal cheek. What I choose to do with my life has nothing at all to do with you. If I want to burn my skin to a crisp, then so I shall.'

'And if you want to be bitten by a thousand mosquitoes you won't care about that either?' He touched a swelling on her shoulder which had been driving her mad all day. No matter how much insect repellent she sprayed on, she always seemed to get bitten.

She shrugged off his hand and slid down into her sleeping-bag, deliberately turning her back on him. 'I'm going to sleep. Goodnight, Braden.'

'Goodnight, Charley.' His voice was soft in her ear, and she tensed when she felt his mouth on the soft skin behind it. Sensations which for days she had resolutely quelled came rushing to the surface, and her whole body ached to be taken into his arms. The romance he had spoken of so scathingly could develop right here if it had a chance. This man was the magic he referred to. He created more excitement inside her than she had ever felt before in her whole life.

But determinedly she lay still and eventually he moved and she heard him wriggle into his sleeping-bag. Within seconds he was asleep. Obviously no such magic had entered his soul. He was a rough, tough man who got his satisfaction and excitement from discovering a culture that had existed hundreds of years ago. What was happening today, what was happening right here in this tent, meant nothing to him at all.

CHAPTER SIX

BRADEN was right when he said Spencer Blake would not be at the Indian encampment. Charley was devastated when she heard that he had not even passed through. 'I knew we'd come the wrong way,' she stormed, so angry she could have hit him. 'We should have taken that other route. We'd have been almost there by now. God, why did I listen to you?'

'Not necessarily,' clipped Braden with ill-concealed impatience. 'Your father probably skirted this camp. They're not particularly friendly, as you've seen.'

Indeed they weren't. Jorge had given his customary yodel as they approached, and almost at once they had been surrounded by Indians with bows and arrows. It had taken Braden a long time to persuade them that they meant no harm. And it had been impossible to get to see their *Sinchi Kooto*. They did discover, though, that he had been their leader for several years.

'All this way for nothing.' Charley was beside herself with rage and frustration, and she bounced up and down angrily on the balls of her feet, her nostrils flaring and her face paper-white. 'I could kill you.'

'That will make you feel better, will it?'

There was tension in Braden's face too, but Charley did not think it was because they had no news of Spencer. It was her attitude that was infuriating him. But what did he expect? She expelled her breath through gritted teeth.

'Damn you. I'll never listen to you again.'

'And damn you, Charley Blake,' he retorted savagely, his eyes gleaming like molten silver. 'Your mother put her trust in me. If you have no faith then I suggest you let me carry on while you turn around and go home.'

'You know that's impossible,' she snapped.

'Then shut up and we'll continue our journey.'

'You still intend to carry on the way we're going?' she demanded.

'That's right.'

'You're not going to cut across and save us a hell of a trek?'

'It would be a hell of a trek if we went the way you're suggesting. You'd never make it. The climbs are too hazardous.'

Charley felt tempted to say that she bet she could, but that would be foolhardy. Instead she shrugged and turned away from him. All those miles they had covered—and the miles that lay ahead. All for nothing. It was a dispiriting thought. Her shoulders sagged and she felt suddenly drained.

When Braden's hand touched her shoulder she whirled around, her eyes flashing.

'I'm sad, too,' he said. 'I didn't think we'd find Spencer, but I did think we'd have some news. I'm sorry, Charley.'

'And what good will being sorry do?' she charged, pulling away from him. 'It won't bring my father any nearer.'

He looked nto the angry coldness of her eyes. 'Don't show your immaturity, Charley, by blaming me.'

'Immature?' she screamed. 'That's one thing you cannot accuse me of being.'

'Then stop harping about something that's nobody's fault, and let's get on with the task of finding your father.'

Their eyes met and locked for several seconds, and for once Charley felt no thrill of excitement. Pure anger was running through her veins. At this moment she hated Braden Quest with every fibre of her being.

In the end she swung away and, grabbing Stalwart's halter, began marching on ahead. Every step she took was tempered with fury, and the mule, sensing her mood, suddenly came to an abrupt halt, and no amount of pulling or persuasion on her part could get him going again.

The fact that Jorge and Coyaso were grinning, and Braden also was doing his best to hide his amusement, did nothing to assuage Charley's temper. She glared at the three of them. 'I don't know what you find so funny. I'll bet none of you can do any better. Stalwart's got it into his head that he doesn't want to go and I don't blame him. You've brought us on a fool's errand.'

Without saying a word Braden took hold of Stalwart's rope, patting the mule encouragingly, murmuring something that made no sense at all to Charley. But the animal moved forward and the two Indian youths fell to the floor laughing. Charley boiled inside and refused to look at Braden as they continued their journey.

The days that followed were filled with tension. Charley still blamed Braden for bringing them the wrong way, and Braden made it clear he thought her reaction totally uncalled for. The atmosphere at night when they were lying in their sleeping-bags was unbearable. Charley could not sleep and she knew

that Braden often lay awake too, but she refused to
speak to him. It was an unbearable situation.

Then one day they topped a rise and found themselves on the outskirts of another Indian camp. They
had not expected it and had not announced their
presence in the usual manner, and Charley clapped a
hand to her mouth in apprehension. She knew how
dangerous it could be to stumble into an Indian camp
without warning.

Braden said something swiftly to Jorge, who
replied that in all truthfulness he had never travelled
this way before and had not known about this village.

Charley walked closely behind them, glancing
about her fearfully. The tribe did not look very
friendly, indeed they looked more hostile than any
others they had yet met, wearing metal discs through
their noses and not very much else.

Their progress was halted when a line of these
fearsome Indians blocked their path, and for the next
twenty minutes Braden was involved in a heated
discussion. At one stage he pointed to Charley and
they looked at her, and it was all she could do to
stand her ground. The conversation ended when
they were led through the village with an escort on
either side.

'What's going on?' asked Charley, but Braden did
not answer, and when they finally reached the last of
the wooden huts he stood back for her to precede him
inside.

Charley hung back, thinking she was going to be
held prisoner, and she looked at Braden
questioningly. He gave an almost imperceptible nod.

It took several mintues for her eyes to become
accustomed to the gloom, and then she saw a bed in
the corner with an old man lying on it, the lower half

of his body covered by a blanket, his face turned away
from them. He was apparently asleep, for he did not
move. His hair was white and straggly and his bones
protruded through his papery thin skin. Charley
thought he must be ill. She turned to Braden with a
frown. 'What are we doing here? Are we supposed to
be helping this man?' Though goodness knew what
they could do. He looked as if he were dying.

Braden took her hand and led her closer to the bed.
'It's your father.'

Charley gasped and a cold shiver ran down her
spine. 'What are you saying? That's not my father.
Goodness me, I should——'

Her words were cut off by the thin, wavering voice
of the man lying down. 'Ch-ar-ley?'

Her eyes widened until they almost filled her face.
This couldn't be her father. It couldn't be. She stared
down at the emaciated figure as he slowly turned his
head towards them, then with a cry of anguish she
threw herself down. 'Oh, Daddy. *Daddy!* Oh, God!'
She could hardly recognise him. His eyes were
sunken, his cheeks hollow. He looked as though he
were clinging to life by a tenuous thread.

Why hadn't Braden warned her? Why had he let
her walk into this? She pressed her cheek against her
father's and her tears ran on to his face. Her throat
was tight with emotion and she could not speak.

'I—knew—you—would—come.'

'What happened?' she asked in a choked whisper.
His hair was completely white. It hadn't been like
this when he'd set off. It had been steel-grey for
years. How he must have suffered!

Weakly he moved his head from side to side, his
faded grey eyes hungry on Charley's face. 'I—fell
ill—dysentery. The—Indians—they looked—after—me.'

And not very well, by the look of it. 'You should have turned back while you were able.'

'No—so near. Charley—so near.' The effort of speaking was too much. He closed his eyes and his head sank back against the blanket rolled up for a pillow. He did not seem to be breathing.

Charley felt swift panic. 'Braden?'

He was at her side in an instant, his fingers pressed to her father's pulse. 'He's sleeping,' he said softly.

She stood up and moved slightly away from the bed. 'Why didn't you warn me?'

He shook his head. 'I didn't realise he was this ill. I thought it would be a nice surprise.'

'Some surprise.' She held her hand to her brow. 'What are we going to do? Will antibiotics help?'

'I have some drugs especially for amoebic dysentery. We'll give him those. Then, with plenty of fluids and rest he should start to get better. Lord knows what sort of stuff the Indians have pumped into him. Thank goodness I brought along plenty of water-purifying tablets. We'll take no chances.'

'You think it was drinking contaminated water that made him ill?'

'Not necessarily. It could have been anything in his diet.'

'I always made sure when I was with him,' she whispered brokenly.

He held her to him. 'Charley, don't blame yourself. It's one of those things. It happens.'

'Men die in the jungle,' she said, more to herself than to him.

'Your father won't die. If he doesn't respond to the treatment, I'll go back myself and bring a helicopter out here.'

'But that will take weeks.'

'It shouldn't do. We've already made a trail, don't forget. The going will be easier, and on my own I'll make good time.'

Charley hoped it didn't come to that. She did not relish the idea of being left here with those ferocious-looking Indians. But nor could she leave her father. She looked at him again and her heart ached. He was little more then a skeleton. Fresh tears coursed down her cheeks.

Braden took her face in his hands and wiped the tears away with his thumbs. 'Don't upset yourself, Charley. We'll do all we can.'

'He looks so ill, so close to——'

'Shh!' He put a gentle finger over her lips. 'He'll be fine, especially now you're here. You'll see.'

He led her outside and the brilliant sunshine hurt her eyes. She sat on the step outside the hut while he unloaded his medical kit from the mule. Jorge and Coyaso touched her shoulder, offering their silent sympathy. A crowd of Indians stood watching.

She followed Braden back in and watched as he gently woke her father. There was a frown on Spencer's face as he focused on the other man. 'Charley?' he asked fraily.

'It's all right, Spencer, she's here.'

'Who—are—you?'

Braden smiled. 'Don't you remember me? Braden Quest. We met in Ecuador a few years ago.'

'Yes—I—remember. You came—together—to look—for—me?'

'That's right.'

'Very—kind.'

'Kind be damned,' said Braden strongly. 'I was persuaded by two very attractive women—your wife and your daughter.'

A ghost of a smile hovered on Spencer's thin lips. 'They were—worried?'

'Like hell. Your daughter blames herself.'

'Charley?' Spencer tried to move his head to look for her, but the effort was too much.

'I'm here, Daddy,' she said, moving towards him, stemming the tears that threatened to overflow again.

'I—love—you.'

'And I love you, Daddy.'

'You're not—to—blame.'

'I am, *I am!*' she cried. 'I should have stopped you from coming. Rupert Billings had no right filling your head with fairy-tales.'

'No—it—is—true. Braden—tell her—over the——' His voice faded as the effort became too great and again he lost consciousness.

'He's not in his right mind,' said Charley, looking sadly down at her father. 'He can't tell me that he was on the verge of discovering the lost city. It's happened so many times. And when we get there, what do we find? A city, yes, but one that's already been discovered. I don't believe that there are any hidden cities left. Not now. Too many people have been looking for too long.'

'I wouldn't say it's impossible,' said Braden gently. 'Highly unlikely, yes, but not altogether impossible. Let's go outside and pitch our tent.'

'The Indians don't mind us staying?'

He must have noticed her apprehension, for he laughed. 'They're not as hostile as they seem. They wouldn't have looked after your father if they were.'

'I'd like to sleep in here with him.'

Braden looked at the hut made of saplings with its mud floor and open doorway. 'I suppose you could,' he said, 'but it offers no protection against mosquitoes and the like. You'll be better off in the tent.'

'If my father can stand it, then so can I,' she protested, though a shudder ran through her.

'Spencer's in no fit state to mind where he is.'

Charley thought about the rat she had seen on that first night and decided that Braden was right. She wouldn't get any sleep for fear of what might be crawling over her. 'OK,' she said reluctantly. 'I'll sleep in the tent, but only if we can pitch it right outside the door.'

Later Charley managed to persuade her father to take a few mouthfuls of soup, but she was desperately worried about him. Most certainly he wouldn't have lived longer than a few more days if they hadn't arrived, but would Braden's medicine work? He needed hospital treatment, but he was too ill and too weak to be moved. He would never survive the journey, even if they could airlift him out right now.

When Charley went to bed that night, she lay awake for long hours thinking about him. And about her mother, too, who did not know what was happening. She must be half out of her mind with worry. Not only was her husband missing, but her daughter was facing danger as well. Isobel Blake had never said how much she worried when they were away, but Charley knew she did. It was there in her face when they got home, the relief, the silent prayer she offered up because they had safely returned.

'Charley, you must get some sleep,' Braden's voice broke into her thoughts.

She was surprised because she thought he had dropped off ages ago. 'I know, but my mind's too active. Poor Daddy. I wish—how I wish we'd found him sooner. I can't see us ever getting him home.'

'We will,' said Braden. 'It will be a long, slow

job bringing him back to good health, but we'll manage it.'

'You sound so confident. I can't help thinking that it's too late. I wish I hadn't left it so long before deciding to search for him.'

'You weren't to know he was ill.'

'I knew something was wrong.'

'No, you didn't. For all you knew he had found his lost city.'

'It's true,' admitted Charley with a wry smile into the darkness, 'I did think that. But I should have known he wouldn't alarm us unnecessarily. If he'd found it he'd have returned and then gone back another time, taking me with him.'

There was silence for a while as they both tried to sleep, then Braden said, 'Charley.'

'Yes?'

'Do you think it might help if I held you?'

Charley closed her eyes and knew that Braden's arms would indeed be a comfort. 'I think so,' she whispered.

'Come here, then.'

So she climbed out of her sleeping-bag and into his, and the hard length of him against her brought a surge of feelings that had been pushed into the background for the last few days.

For a moment Charley felt faint unease that he might have an ulterior motive, but when he pulled her head into his shoulder, and murmured words of comfort as he stroked her hair, she began to relax, and within minutes was asleep.

When she awoke it was daylight and she was still cocooned against him. She felt warm and relaxed, and when she ventured to look at his face he was awake too and he smiled at her. But when she tried to struggle out of his arms his hold on her tightened.

'Let me go, Braden,' she said quietly but firmly. 'I must see how my father is.'

'A few more minutes won't hurt. I like you against me.'

And in all honesty Charley liked being close to him, too. She could feel the full, hard length of his legs, and the firmness of his body, and his hair-roughened chest. If it weren't for the fact that she was so anxious about her father she would have revelled in these moments spent together.

He touched a finger to her face, outlining her nose and her lips, stroking across her cheekbones and eyelids, and the look in his eyes was softer than it had ever been before.

But Charley knew the insanity of remaining here. They were both too aware of each other's bodies. How long he had been awake she did not know, but he was a virile male and it must be hell holding her, having her so close, yet doing nothing about it.

She admired his restraint. Not many men in his position would treat her so respectfully. She moved unconsciously against him and he groaned. 'I wonder if you know what you're doing to me?'

'I have an idea,' she whispered, and lifted her face to look at him.

His mouth on hers was pure torment, sending a torrent of feelings right through the very heart of her. Against her will she parted her lips and let him deepen the kiss, and for a few delirious seconds she forgot her cares.

He pulled down her lower lip and kissed the soft moist flesh inside. He trailed his fingers lightly down the slender column of her throat, pausing on her fluttering pulse, then slowly moving over the fullness of her breasts. His touch was tantalisingly light, moving in ever-decreasing circles until only the rosy aureole remained untouched. And how she ached for him.

'Braden,' she prompted, arching herself against him, aware of his arousal, but a little frightened too.

'Mmm?'

'Braden, don't tease me so.'

'What is it you want?'

Her nipple was suddenly pinched by his thumb and forefinger, making her gasp with sheer un-expected pleasure. And as she opened her mouth Braden's closed over it yet again, his tongue urgent now, his hand on her breast no longer gentle.

When he finally dragged his mouth away from hers his breathing was harsh. 'I think, Charley, you'd better get up. I won't be responsible for my actions if you stay any longer.'

Nor would she. Already she was losing her sanity. She wanted him to go on kissing her, to go on touching and inciting her. But she could see the wisdom behind his words.

She climbed out of the sleeping-bag and he watched her as she dressed. Charley had long since lost any embarrassment, but today she knew that her naked body was affecting him, and it gave her an extra feeling of satisfaction.

She was unzipping the flap on the tent when she felt Braden's arms about her waist. She had not heard him get up and he startled her. He turned her around and held her close. 'I think I must be a little foolish to let you go. You're quite a woman, Charley. Quite a woman.'

The next moment he was pushing her out, and

Charley forgot about him when she entered her father's hut.

Spencer Blake's eyes were on the door, watching for her, but he looked no better, and it broke her heart seeing him lying there so still and frail.

'Hello, Dad.'

'It—wasn't—a—dream?'

She smiled and bent over him and kissed his cheek. 'No dream. I'm here, and as soon as you're better I'm taking you home.'

'I don't—think—I will—get—better.'

Charley ached inside. 'Nonsense. Braden has something that will cure you. We'll have you right in no time at all.'

'You're—so—good. I couldn't—have—wished—for a—better—daughter.'

'You've forgiven me for not being a boy?' she jested smilingly.

'No—son—could have—given me—more—pleasure. How—is—Isobel?'

'She's worried, naturally,' said Charley, 'but she's fine. I wish there was some way of getting a message to her.'

'I—I don't—know—how—long—I've—been—here.'

'Too long,' smiled Charley.

'The—Indians—are—good.'

She nodded.

'I would—have—died—without—them.'

'I'll ask Braden to thank them. He speaks fluent Quechua.' She kissed her father's brow. 'I'm going to find a spring where I can wash, and then I'll be back and I'll spend the whole day with you. Braden will be here in a little while with your medicine.'

Tears were in her eyes as she left him, and she hurried through her toilet. When she got back,

Braden was with him.

During the days that followed they coaxed him with soup made from their powdered supply, boiled in fresh water from the spring but with a water-purifying tablet added just in case. Charley squeezed pints of orange juice from fresh oranges—she knew that fruit with a peel was always free from contamination—and gradually he regained some of his strength. He was able to sit up with their help and he said he was feeling much better.

He enquired about the Indians who had been his guides and were supposed to fetch help. 'No one's heard anything,' said Charley. 'My mother and I were at our wits' end. I wish we hadn't left it so long.' She privately doubted that he would be able to gain enough strength to make the long and arduous journey home.

One night in their tent she voiced her fears.

'I agree with you,' Braden said. 'I think it would be best if I went back and arranged an airlift. Your father needs hospital treatment.'

'I don't want to be left here alone,' she said in a tight little voice.

'It's the only way,' he replied. 'What's happened to you, Charley? Where's that brave woman who set out on this journey? "What a man can do I can do," isn't that what you said? You have no choice. You'll have to wait here with your father.' Then he grinned. 'Unless you go back and I'll wait.'

A look of horror crossed her face. 'I'm sorry. Of course you must go.'

'You still have Jorge and Coyaso. They'll help you all they can.'

'If only I could speak Quechua.'

'You're not doing too badly. I've seen your sign

language. It's pretty good. I'll set off in the morning. You continue to give your father his medicine, and try and wean him on to solids, and by the time I come back he should be up to the flight.'

'OK,' she said, swallowing hard.

'Come here.'

They were sitting cross-legged on top of their sleeping-bags and since that first night he had not kissed her again. Charley crept over to him and he held her close. 'You're not really as tough as you make out, are you?'

She shook her head.

'It's a relief, do you know that? I don't like masculine women.'

She gave a tremulous smile. The light from the lamp cast shadows across his face and his blonde hair looked much darker. He needed a shave, too. She touched his chin with her finger and wondered why he had never grown a beard. It would have suited him. It would have hidden his scar, too.

'I like my women soft and feminine. I like them to melt in my arms——' As she was doing now! 'I like them to wear pretty clothes and have long hair.' As he spoke he released her hair from its confining band and teased the braids out until they hung silken and heavy about her shoulders. He ran the hair through his fingers and buried his nose in it. 'Mmm, it smells beautiful.'

'Like a mountain stream?' she smiled. She had washed it that morning while he was in with her father.

'It's a heady perfume. I'd like to bottle it and take it home, and every time I smelled it, it would remind me of you.'

Charley's eyes widened. Was this really Braden talking such nonsense?

'What's wrong?' he asked.

'I've never known you like this.'

His mouth twisted wryly. 'I'm not always a bully.' He lowered his head and kissed her mouth. 'In fact, I can be quite romantic. But not tonight. When I make love to you, the time and place will have to be exactly right.'

'When you—make love to me?' Charley husked, going hot at the thought.

'That's right. It's what we both want, isn't it?'

'I—don't know. I——'

He silenced her with another kiss, and Charley's arms snaked instinctively around the back of his neck. Yes, it was what she wanted, very much. But it went against every vow she had ever made. And Braden didn't love her. He had not mentioned one word of love. He desired her, that was all. She pulled herself free.

He smiled. 'Goodnight, Charley. Go to bed now. And I must get some sleep, too, if I'm to begin my journey tomorrow.'

Charley crawled into her sleeping-bag. 'How long do you think it will take?' And her body ached to be possessed by him.

'A couple of weeks at the very least, I imagine.'

'I'll miss you.'

'And me you.' He slid into his own bed. 'I didn't want to bring you with me, Charley, you know that, but I have to admire your guts. I doubt if I'll ever meet anyone else like you.'

And she knew that she would never meet anyone else like Braden. If he walked out of her life once they got her father home, then she would remain single for ever. No other man would match up to him. No matter what she told herself, she loved Braden, and she always would.

CHAPTER SEVEN

THE days dragged after Braden left the Indian camp. Charley spent most of her time with her father, talking to him, feeding him, washing him. He did not seem to grow any stronger and she was deeply worried. His skin was stretched tightly across his skeletal frame. Even the effort of sitting up was too much, and Charley began to doubt whether he would get well enough for the long journey to England.

They could, of course, take him to hospital in Lima, but she knew that her father would rather go home. And she would prefer that, too. There was something comforting about being in your native country.

The nights were the worst. She lay awake in her tent and wished Braden was with her. Although the Indians weren't hostile, they weren't over-friendly, either. They viewed her from a distance, only the children coming anywhere near. Jorge and Coyaso were her go-betweens, and she did not know what she would have done without them.

Her father spoke about the lost city. 'It breaks my heart to know that we're so near.'

'You still believe Rupert Billings' tale?' It was difficult to keep the scepticism out of her voice.

'Of course. And I shall be back. All my life I've dreamt of finding the lost city of the Incas. I can't give up now.'

'I'll come with you next time,' she said softly, and did not remind him that only a few days ago he had

115

said he would not live.

He put his hand over hers. 'I love you, Charley.'

The blue veins were prominent on the back of his hand, his skin almost translucent. Charley held him and felt like crying. Her father had always been so strong and active, a very fit man for his age, and she could not bear to see him like this.

Every day she watched out for Braden to return, and every night she went to bed and prayed. Sixteen days went by before she heard the unmistakable throb of a helicopter. Jorge and Coyaso had already warned the Indians what to expect, and had helped clear an area where Braden could land.

Charley ran towards it, and as soon as Braden climbed down she flung herself at him. She did not care what he thought. It had been the longest two weeks of her life.

His arms were comforting around her. She felt as though she belonged and that this was her rightful place. It was a ridiculous thought, but she could not help it.

He finally held her at arm's length. 'Your father—how is he?' His face was grave.

Did he think her enthusiasm in seeing him was because her father was worse? 'He's improved a little, but not much,' she said. 'I'm so afraid.'

'We'll soon have him in the right hands. This is Dr Lago. He's come with me to check on your father before we move him.'

Charley had not noticed the other man. Now she turned and saw a small, dark-skinned man with gold-rimmed glasses and a shining bald head. She held out her hand. 'Thank you for coming. I'm very grateful.'

'Let me look at your father,' he said.

'Of course.' Charley led the way to her father's hut and a crowd of curious Indian children followed.

The doctor gave Spencer Blake a thorough examination while Charley looked on anxiously. She clutched Braden's hand almost without realising it. 'He doesn't look much better, does he?' she whispered.

He squeezed her fingers. 'He's alive, Charley, that's the main thing.'

After he had finished examining Spencer, the doctor commended them. 'If you hadn't found him when you did and given him the right medicine, then I don't think he would be alive today.'

'I have Braden to thank for that,' Charley said, tears in her eyes. Had she gone with Alan they would have taken a different route, she knew that. Alan would have listened to her. And she would have been wrong. *And her father would have died!*

Braden's lips twisted. 'I did what any man would have done under the circumstances.'

'Can Daddy go home to England?' she asked the doctor hopefully.

But he shook his head. 'I'm afraid not. He'd never make the journey. It will be as much as he can take flying to Lima. But do not worry, we have a fine hospital there. We will bring him back to good health.'

Charley nodded sadly. She was disappointed but she had half expected it.

'Come on, Charley,' said Braden, 'let's pack up and get out of here.'

With Jorge and Coyaso's help their kit was soon stowed on board the helicopter and her father carefully lifted on to a stretcher. With handshakes all round and gifts of Braden's shirts to the two Indian boys, who now faced the long trek back to their own camp, they took off.

Dr Lago kept a careful eye on Spencer, while Braden and Charley sat and talked. At Cuzco they changed to a waiting plane. Spencer drifted in and out of consciousness during the flight, and it was easy to see that he would never have stood up to a further fifteen or so hours in the air.

Once he was settled in hospital Charley phoned her mother who broke down and cried, then said she would be with her as soon as possible.

'And now,' said Braden, 'home and a much needed bath.'

Charley felt sad. Despite their inauspicious start, she had grown to love this sometimes ruthless, sometimes surprising man. She would miss him, she would miss him terribly. 'I appreciate all you've done, Braden,' she said with a sad smile. 'I don't know how I can ever repay you.'

'I have a few ideas about that,' he said, 'but we won't discuss them here and now. Come on, Carlos is waiting.'

Charley frowned. She had assumed this was the end of the road as far as they were concerned. 'Where are you taking me?'

'Home, of course.'

'But that's not necessary,' she said, ignoring the sudden quickening of her pulses. 'Your job is finished. I'm going to book into a hotel.'

Braden's thick black brows rose. 'Charley! I've three or four rooms sitting empty, what's the point?' He picked up her haversack and began to walk away. 'Your mother can stay at my place, too,' he flung over his shoulder.

She was left with little alternative but to follow, and

her stupid heart was banging fit to burst. It was the last thing she had expected.

Nevertheless it was heaven to soak in a scented bath and wash her hair in hot water straight from a tap. These were luxuries that were taken for granted in the civilised world. And how she had missed them.

She had towel-dried her hair and pulled on her cleanest shirt and trousers when Braden walked in. They had spent so much time living together it never entered Charley's head to tell him off for intruding on her privacy. He wore a pair of pale blue trousers and a white shirt, and he looked magnificent. Not a bit tired, not in the least as though he had just completed a marathon trip through the jungle. His hair had grown in the weeks they had been away and it suited him.

In contrast Charley felt drained and scruffy. 'Can I do some washing?' she asked, looking down at her stained trousers doubtfully. 'My mother's bringing me some things, but I can't go around looking like this in the meantime.'

'My housekeeper will do it,' he said dismissively. 'But you know I prefer you in something more feminine. I think I can find you a dress or two to tide you over.'

Charley frowned. 'Of course. Every man keeps a wardrobe of ladies' clothes just in case.'

His lips quirked. 'Actually, they belong to a friend. I'm sure she won't mind you borrowing them.'

A friend, who left her clothes here? Charley felt a flash of jealousy which she squashed at once. Braden's private life was nothing to do with her. But, as for wearing this unknown girl's clothes, that was a different story.

'Thanks for the offer, but no. I'll manage.'

His mouth tightened in annoyance. 'If you're going

to work for me, I don't want you looking like that.'

'Work for you?' Charley's eyes grew wide in astonishment. 'What are you talking about?'

'A little recompense for my time and effort.' There was sudden suspicious innocence on his face.

So that was why he had offered to put her up. It wasn't out of the kindness of his heart. And he had said he didn't want payment! 'I intend spending as much time as possible with my father,' she announced with a haughty toss of her head. 'I'm sorry, but——'

'Your father will tire easily for a while,' he said. 'He won't be strong enough for long visits. And your mother will be here soon, so you'll have no excuse.'

Charley met the silver challenge in his eyes. 'What kind of work?' she asked coolly. 'I have no particular qualifications.'

'I'm well aware of that,' he smiled, 'but none are needed. And it's something you'll enjoy, so you needn't get all uptight about it.'

'Oh, yes,' she flashed. 'I'll enjoy working for you as much as I'd enjoy having my leg chopped off.'

'Such enthusiasm,' he mocked. 'Somehow I got the impression that you were sad we were parting. I thought you might welcome the opportunity of spending a little more time with me. Was I wrong?'

Charley felt sudden heat prickle her skin. Had she been so transparent? 'Very wrong,' she lied loudly. 'I appreciate what you've done, but really, the way you treated me while we were searching for my father, I'd need my head examining if I wanted to hang around.'

A muscle jerked in his jaw and the amused mockery disappeared. 'I did what I had to do. If I'd made allowances because of your sex, it might have been too late by the time we found your father.'

Charley's blue eyes were resentful. 'You could have used less merciless methods.'

'I treated you the same as I would any member of such an expedition. If you took exception, that's your fault.'

He was making sense, but even so Charley found it difficult to forgive him. Only at the end had he been kind. She shrugged and eyed him resentfully. 'What is it, this work you want me to do?'

His face was tight now, with none of the indulgence he had shown earlier. But that had only been because he wanted something, she told herself fiercely, and she was glad she hadn't given in without a fight. To be truthful, she wanted nothing that would throw them together. There was no point in loving a man who felt no affection in return. His interest had been purely sexual. A clean break was best.

'I have a lot of research for my new book that needs putting into some sort of order. Neither Ramón nor I have time to do it.'

Charley's brow furrowed. 'Who's Ramón?'

'He's doing the artwork. You'll meet him tomorrow.'

She felt a stirring of interest. 'What's your book about?'

'The Incas, of course.'

'Is there anything left to write about them?' she asked in surprise.

'This is different,' he said. 'I've been approached by the education authorities, who want to make the history of the Inca empire more enjoyable for the younger children.'

'I see,' said Charley, her interest deepening by the second. 'How are you going to do that?'

'There is only one way.' The hard angles left his face. This was a subject he loved passionately. 'I shall write it from an Inca's point of view.'

Her fine brows rose. 'You think you'll be able to put yourself into the part?'

'Most definitely. Ironically, my grandfather was Spanish, and according to him one of our antecedents was among the conquistadors led into Peru in the fifteen-thirties by Francisco Pizarro.'

'So why don't you write it from a conquistador's point of view?'

'Because I damn well don't agree with what they did,' he snorted. 'It was the beginning of the end of the Inca empire.'

Charley nodded, agreeing with him whole-heartedly. She wondered what sort of a role he would put himself into. It should be interesting to find out.

'And if you won't wear Estefa's dresses then we'll go shopping right now to get you something else.'

His sudden change of topic confused Charley. She looked at him for a blank moment, then said sharply, 'I haven't money for that sort of thing.'

'My treat.'

'I already owe you,' she thrust back. 'If you can't bear to see me in trousers for a couple of days then hard luck.'

Again his brow darkened, but he let her challenge pass. 'Juanita has a meal waiting. After that I imagine we'll both be ready for bed.'

'I want to see my father,' protested Charley strongly. Why was he forever trying to rule her life?

'He's probably still asleep.' Braden's clipped tones gave away his impatience. 'You'd be wasting your time. The flight took a lot out of him, don't forget.'

She nodded. He was right as usual, damn him. Her
father had looked as if he would barely make the
journey. But at least he was in good hands. He would
never have survived out there in the jungle, even
with their care. 'I'll go tomorrow,' she said quietly.

The meal was delicious. *Choclos*, to start with,
tender maize cobs served with cheese, followed by
asado, lean beef covered with garlic butter, puréed
fresh tomatoes and chilli, then casseroled until
tender, served with *puré de papas*, runny mashed
potatoes whipped up with butter and garlic.

Charley refused a dessert. She sat back, replete.
'My compliments to your housekeeper.'

'It beats dried soup and turtle eggs?' There was
faint humour in his words. The meal seemed to have
soothed his temper.

'Any day,' she agreed, stretching her arms above
her head and yawning.

His silver-grey eyes rested intently on her face. 'I'll
miss you tonight, Charley. I got quite used to you
sharing my tent.'

Trying her hardest to ignore the excitement such a
thought caused, Charley's tone was unintentionally
sharp. 'I hope that's not a hint you'd like me to share
your bedroom? If that's behind the suggestion, then
you can forget the whole thing. I'll book into a hotel.'
She scraped back her chair and stood up. 'There's no
way I'm going to let you touch me again.'

'You're protesting too much, Charley,' he said,
admirably controlling the flicker of temper she had
seen in his eyes. 'But actually I think we're both too
tired to appreciate each other tonight.'

He draped his arm about her shoulders as they
made their way upstairs and, light though his touch
was, it felt like a branding-iron. Outside her bedroom

door he stopped and turned her to face him. He bent his head and kissed her lightly on the mouth. 'Goodnight, Charley.'

She had expected more, had indeed wanted more, and felt acute disappointment as he walked away. 'Goodnight, Braden,' she whispered. *I'll miss you, too.*

But the instant her head hit the pillow she was asleep, and when she opened her eyes again it was broad daylight. The windows were flung wide—though she knew they had been closed last night, and a breeze billowed the curtains into the room. She glanced at her watch then sprang out of bed in consternation. It was almost midday. Why hadn't Braden woken her? Her father must think she didn't care.

Washing quickly she looked for her clothes. They were missing—all of them. There were a couple of dresses on hangers and a few pairs of briefs in their original packaging, but that was all. Her lips clamped. *Very funny, Braden. Very funny, indeed.*

She pulled on one of the offending dresses and dragged a brush angrily through her hair; then, without even looking in the mirror, she ran downstairs.

The housekeeper met her, smiling broadly. '*Buenos días, señorita.* You sleep well, *si?*'

'Yes, yes,' said Charley impatiently. 'Where is Braden?'

'He go to the hospital. He be back soon,' beamed Juanita.

'To the hospital?' echoed Charley disbelievingly. 'Without me?'

'He say not to wake you. You need sleep.'

'I need to see my father,' she exploded. 'Is Carlos here?'

'No, he take Señor Quest,' shrugged the house-keeper, looking upset by Charley's questioning. 'Lo siento, I did not know. I only do what he say.'

'It's not your fault,' said Charley. 'I'm just so worried about my father. Can you order me a taxi?'

The woman nodded. 'Si, but first you must eat.'

'I'm not hungry,' objected Charley.

'The señor, he say——'

'I don't care what Braden says,' she cried. 'I want to see my father before I do anything else.'

'Your father has enjoyed a good night and is now resting peacefully.' Braden's amused voice came from behind her. Charley whirled around. 'And he said to make sure you were fully rested yourself before you considered visiting him.'

'And you should know what I think about that suggestion,' she snapped. 'Why didn't you wake me?'

'You were sleeping like a baby,' he said with a satisfied smile.

So it was he who had opened her window! Charley's anger knew no bounds. 'I'd thank you not to come uninvited into my room again.'

His brows rose. 'My, my, we are in a temper.'

'Of course I'm angry,' she flared. 'You know how badly I want to see my father. Why did you go? What's he to you?'

A flicker of impatience crossed Braden's face. 'He's the man I've spent three long weeks searching for, that's what he is to me. What did you think, that once I'd found him I'd dismiss him? A job well done and all that? Have a heart, Charley. I'm not quite that callous.'

'You could have fooled me,' she muttered beneath her breath, then on a more anxious note, 'Is my father really all right?'

Braden nodded. 'Very weak, naturally, but no worse. He'll pull through.'

'When can I go and see him?'

'Carlos will take you tonight.'

'But——'

'But nothing,' he said firmly. 'If you're feeling at a loose end I can find you plenty to do.'

'As if I could concentrate,' she fumed, 'when my father's——'

'In the best possible hands,' he cut in brutally.

'None of this would have happened if you'd let me book into a hotel,' she accused. 'I could have come and gone as I pleased, instead of being a virtual prisoner.'

'You're not a prisoner,' he pointed out.

'No? You could have fooled me. I'm told when to go to bed, when to visit my father. I even have my clothes taken off me. Damn you, Braden Quest. I hate you.'

He grinned. 'I thought the dress looked rather stunning myself. It suits you.'

It suited his taste, more likely. It was a vibrant yellow, and although it fitted her it was too revealing, with shoestring straps and a low-cut neckline. Not the sort of thing she normally wore. Braden seemed unable to take his eyes off her.

'As I had an early breakfast I'm just about ready for lunch,' he announced with some satisfaction. 'We'll eat together. Juanita?'

His housekeeper nodded and rushed off to do his bidding. Charley fumed silently and followed him through the house. It was a shock when he pushed open a heavy door and she was confronted by an indoor swimming-pool.

'I had no idea,' she said, her eyes widening. She
had thought they were entering the dining-room. It
was exotic to say the least, with aqua tiles and potted
plants and palms and brightly coloured loungers.

'A necessity in Lima, as far as I'm concerned. Peru
is a country of contrasts, as you know, and thanks to
the Humboldt Current the ocean at this point is cool
at the best of times. Most of the locals wear wetsuits.
In any case, it's a long jaunt and I like a swim before
breakfast. And as it's such a nice morning I don't
think we need this.' He pressed a button and the
glass roof slid slowly and silently out of
sight.

Charley was impressed. Apart from the four
summer months of December to April, Lima was
often shrouded in a thick, heavy blanket of mist.
What a good idea this was. It gave him the best of
both worlds.

He began peeling off his shirt. 'I missed my swim
today. Are you joining me?'

Charley shook her head.

He was down to his underpants now and she
turned her head away, but when she heard the
splash as he dived into the water she looked and saw
the long nude shape of him.

She ought not to feel shy, she had stripped off in
front of him in the tent more than once, but somehow
it was different here. This was civilisation, and
civilised people did not parade naked in front of each
other.

He streaked to the far end of the pool, executed a
perfect turn, then swam back towards her. His body
was tanned and sleek and powerful, and she could
not take her eyes off him. 'I'm waiting,' he said,
drawing level and hanging on to the side. 'What's

wrong, can't you swim?'

'Of course I can swim,' she replied indignantly.

'You're afraid I might show you up?'

'No.'

'It's because it's so near to lunch time?'

'No!' she protested. 'I just don't want to.'

'Liar,' he taunted. 'I know what's wrong. You're afraid of me seeing you without your clothes on. If you had a swimsuit, you wouldn't hesitate. Isn't that so?'

His brows rose in a wicked arch when she did not answer. 'I could oblige. There's a couple of Estefa's bikinis lying around somewhere, but for what use they are you might as well not bother.'

'I wouldn't wear one of hers, anyway,' she told him haughtily. 'I wouldn't even be wearing this dress if I'd had any choice. It was a despicable thing to do. I'm going up to my room. You can call me when lunch is ready.'

She turned round and did not realise he had hauled himself out of the pool. Not until she felt his arms about her was Charley aware of any danger. 'Braden, put me down!' she yelled. 'How dare you——' The next second she was sailing through the air. The water rushed up to meet her and she hit the surface with a mighty splash.

Surfacing, she tossed her hair out of her eyes and looked angrily around for Braden. He was treading water at her side, a devilish grin creasing his face. 'Really, Charley, you should know by now that I never take no for an answer.'

'You wait,' she thrust savagely. 'I'll get my own back.'

'I'm sure you'll try,' he said, 'but don't be too sure about succeeding. Meantime, let's have a race.' He set off, but the dress hampered Charley's movements and in the end she wriggled out of it. He was waiting at the other end of the pool. 'Some performance.' And he did not mean her swimming.

'Damn you,' she grated.

'You're beautiful when you're angry.' He hooked his leg around hers, and then his arms, and Charley found herself imprisoned against him. It was impossible to ignore the sensations caused by his hard, cool body, and to be truthful she did not want to.

She had thought, when they found her father and returned to Lima, that it would be the end of their relationship. She had resigned herself to the fact. This was an added bonus. Instead of fighting him she ought to take what he offered and store it carefully in her mind, to be brought out and relived whenever she felt a need for him back home in England.

His mouth found hers and she responded without conscious thought. It was a cruel fate that had made her fall in love with a man who had no long-lasting interest in her.

The kiss went on and on and Charley arched herself even closer. The wild throb of her heart threatened to deafen her. Could he feel it against his chest? She was aware of his heart beating faster than normal, but that did not mean his feelings went any deeper than simple desire. Men were able to conduct an affair without involving their emotions. It was something she could not do. To need and desire a man meant she had to love him too.

Suddenly Braden struck away from the side, taking her with him, and they swam like fish, their bodies entwined, their mouths clinging except when they needed to draw breath. It was an exhilarating experience. Charley wondered how long it would have gone on if they hadn't been interrupted.

'I hate to disturb you two, but Juanita is complaining about lunch being spoilt.'

Charley looked up and and saw a swarthy-skinned, good-looking man grinning down at them. He was dressed in pale grey trousers and a yellow half-sleeved shirt which in no way hid his powerful physique.

'Ramón, you old devil, I didn't expect you today.'

'Obviously,' came the smiling response.

Feeling a little embarrassed at being caught like this, Charley struggled to free herself, but Braden had other ideas. His arms about her tightened. 'Ramón, meet Charley Blake, the girl I told you about. Charley, Ramón El Gordo, my artistic partner.'

'You didn't say what a stunner she was.' The newcomer's eyes were genuinely admiring. 'Hello, Charley. I can see this is suddenly going to be a much nicer place in which to work.'

'Don't get the wrong idea,' warned Braden at once, and he sounded almost as though he were jealous, though Charley knew this could not be so.

'Hello, Ramón,' she called out cheerfully. 'Don't be too generous with your compliments. Once I get my hands on your papers you might never find anything again.'

'For you, I will forgive anything,' he said gallantly.

She laughed. 'I promise you I'm an ignoramus when it comes to paperwork. I've only ever served behind a counter.'

'Such modesty,' he smiled. 'From all accounts you are a female explorer *extraordinaire*. I am certainly looking forward to making your acquaintance.'

Was that what Braden had called her? Charley looked at him quickly, but he was frowning at the other man. She took the opportunity to slip out of his grasp and swim for the side. Immediately Ramón's hand was there to haul her out, and too late she realised that all she was wearing was a pair of pink lacy briefs, transparent now they were wet.

But she hid her self-consciousness and tried to pretend that it was perfectly natural to be talking to a stranger in her birthday suit. He was not as tall as Braden and much older, but it did not detract from his masculinity. Not that she was attracted to him in a sexual way, Braden held all her feelings in that respect, but Ramón looked as though he could be interesting and entertaining company. Maybe exactly what she needed to divert her attention away from Braden. It was futile getting too involved when all it would bring was heartache.

'I am sorry to hear about your father,' Ramón was saying. 'I am sure he will soon get better.'

'I hope so,' she said. 'I'm desperately worried.'

'It must be a comfort to him, knowing you are here.'

'Not much, when I haven't been allowed to see him today,' she flashed. 'Braden went this morning without waking me.'

'Then allow me to take you after lunch. It will be my——'

'Charley's going nowhere after lunch,' growled Braden fiercely. He had picked up a towel from somewhere and now he thrust it fiercely at her. 'Cover yourself up, for goodness' sake.'

Ramón looked startled by Braden's attitude. 'If Charley wants to go, then——'

'It's her father I'm thinking of,' he interjected sharply. 'I've already promised to take her tonight. Don't butt in where you're not wanted, Ramón.'

The other man's face flushed a deep red and he looked apologetically at Charley. She lifted her shoulders, equally startled by Braden's harsh words.

Braden touched her arm. 'Let's go and get changed.' And when they were out of Ramón's hearing, 'You can forget him. He's married.'

'I wasn't planning on going to bed with him.' Charley's tone was as keen as his, her eyes aggressive. 'And I'm sure all he was doing was being friendly.'

'Too damned friendly. And you had no right parading yourself in front of him. It's no wonder he got the wrong idea.'

She glared. 'And whose fault is it that I've got nothing on? It's yourself you should criticise. I happen to think Ramón's a very nice guy, and if he offers again to take me to the hospital I shall go.'

'He won't offer,' said Braden confidently.

And Charley did not think he would. Braden's word seemed to be a law around this place.

CHAPTER EIGHT

WHEN Charley arrived at the hospital she was amazed to find her mother sitting at her father's bedside. He was asleep and Isobel looked exhausted and pale, but nevertheless she smiled warmly when she saw her daughter.

'I never expected you to get here so quickly,' said Charley, hugging her tightly and kissing her.

'I managed to get a flight straight away. It was panic stations after you phoned. I never really thought you'd find your father alive. And I was so afraid, after how ill you said he was, that it would be too late when I got here.'

'At one time I didn't think he'd live myself,' admitted Charley. 'I couldn't even recognise him when we found him.' Tears filled her eyes at the memory. 'Oh, God, it was awful.'

'I've spoken to Dr Lago,' said her mother firmly, 'and he has every confidence that your father will pull through. It will be a long, slow job, he's more seriously ill than the doctor first thought, but he told me not to lose hope.'

Charley pulled up another chair and sat down, and they both looked at the shrunken man lying so still beneath the sheets. 'He'll recover,' Charley said. 'He's got a will of iron. He was even talking about going back. He believes he was so close to his precious lost city.'

Isobel nodded sadly, taking Spencer's limp hand in hers. 'It's been a lifelong dream. And if that's what your father said, then I've no doubt that's what he'll do. But I shan't let him go alone, not ever again.'

'Nor will I,' said Charley at once. 'I'll go with him. You don't have to worry about that.'

'You're a good girl, but he needs another man at this stage in his life. Alan, perhaps, though he's talking of getting married, and Julie's not keen on the idea of him leaving her for weeks at a time. Now, if Braden went with him I'd have no fears.'

Charley snorted inelegantly. 'Braden believes, the same as me, that this was a wild-goose chase. He doesn't even believe there is a lost city.'

Isobel Blake frowned at the harsh note in Charley's voice. 'Something tells me you two didn't get on?'

'Sometimes we did, sometimes we didn't,' she shrugged. 'You should have seen the way he treated me. I'm sure he thought I could do a man's work.'

Her mother's lips quirked. 'You weren't slow to point out how experienced you were.'

'Even so, he could have made allowances,' grumbled Charley.

'From what little I've seen of Braden, he's not the type.'

'You can say that again,' stormed Charley. 'If Braden says jump, you jump. Do you know he wouldn't let me come and see Daddy this afternoon? I was asleep this morning when he came visiting, and when I——'

'Wait a minute,' frowned her mother, 'you're losing me. What's this with Braden? He's done the job we asked him to do, what——'

'Of course, you don't know, do you?' cut in Charley with a grimace. 'He's insisting we both stay at his house while Daddy's in hospital.'

'Oh, how kind,' said Isobel Blake at once.

'Kind, my foot. There is a condition.' Her mother's fine brows rose. 'I'm to work for him.'

'Doing what?' asked the older woman in some surprise.

Charley lifted her shoulders. 'Sorting some papers out for his new book.'

Isobel Blake's eyes cleared. 'That should be interesting, love.'

'But I don't want to do it, I don't want to work for him, I don't even want to stay with him.'

'Then why did you agree?'

'Because he gave me no choice. He's that type of man, Mom.'

'He sounds very kind to me. He found your father, and now he's putting us up. The least you can do is help him out. What sort of a book is it?'

'About the Incas,' informed Charley reluctantly.

'There you are then, love. Right up your street. I think it's a marvellous idea.'

At that moment Spencer stirred. 'Isobel?' he whispered, and his eyes filled with tears.

'Spencer.' Isobel Blake got up out of her chair and put her cheek against his. 'Oh, Spencer!'

It was several long seconds before either of them moved, and Charley's throat was tight as she watched their tearful reunion.

'And my brave girl.' Spencer held his hand out towards his daughter, drawing her into the circle of his love. 'How are you feeling? Braden told me you were very tired.'

'But not that tired I didn't want to come and see you. He should have woken me.'

'No,' said her father at once. 'He did the right thing. He's quite a guy, isn't he?' I'll be forever in his debt.'

'Charley's going to help him write his new book,' said her mother proudly.

Spencer's eyes widened.

'Not help him write it, Mom,' laughed Charley. 'He needs some research papers sorting, that sort of thing. I suppose it will be interesting.'

'Suppose?' echoed her father. 'There's no suppose about it. You'll thoroughly enjoy it, you know you will. It's a wonderful opportunity. Almost worth being ill for. Who knows what it could lead to? He might give you a permanent job.'

Charley's chin jutted. 'I wouldn't take it.'

'Why not?' Spencer frowned.

'Because, quite simply, we don't see eye to eye.'

'I don't understand,' said her father.

'It's easy. He doesn't like women who behave like men. He had it in for me from the moment we set out to find you. I hate him.'

They both looked surprised by the vehemence in her tone. 'Are you sure you're not protesting too strongly?' asked her mother.

'And what's that supposed to mean?' snapped Charley.

'If you hate him that much, you wouldn't stay in his house. You're too strong-minded, Charley. You must have wanted to.'

Charley eyed her mother for a long moment. 'OK, so maybe I did. But it's just the job that's attracting me, nothing else.'

'Of course, love,' said her mother.

They stayed until Spencer began to show signs of strain, but even then Isobel was reluctant to leave. 'I'll be here first thing in the morning,' she promised.

Carlos drove them to Braden's mansion in Barranco, and Isobel Blake's eyes widened as they approached. It had grown dark while they were in the hospital and the house was floodlit, making the porticoed frontage look even more dramatic.

As they climbed the flight of steps to the massive front door, Carlos carrying the two suitcases Isobel had brought with her, it swung open, and Braden stood waiting to great them.

It suited him, this fine house, decided Charley. In a pair of beige soft suede trousers, Gucci shoes, and a fine cashmere sweater he was as imposing as his surroundings. It was impossible to control the sudden flip her heart gave. Just looking at him made her want him.

'Isobel,' he smiled, his teeth very white against his tan. 'I had no idea you'd arrived yet. Welcome to my humble abode.'

'Humble?' questioned the older woman with a laugh. 'It's magnificent. I had no idea you lived anywhere like this. It's most kind of you to let Charley and me stay here. I hate hotels.'

'Unlike your daughter.' And there was no disguising the mockery in his tone.

'I wanted to be nearer to Daddy,' she defended herself.

'Do come inside,' he went on. 'Juanita will show you to your room and then get you something to eat. It's a hellish flight from London, isn't it? But I'm sure you'll feel better after a shower.'

'Actually, I'm not hungry,' said Isobel. 'But I am dead tired. I'd like nothing more than to go straight to bed. Would you think that awfully rude?'

'Not in the least, dear lady. Carlos, take these cases up to the room next to Señorita Blake's. And please tell Juanita I want her.'

'The blue case is Charley's,' said Isobel at once.

Braden smiled. 'She'll love you for ever for that, Mrs Blake.' The woman frowned. 'Charley's rather short of suitable clothes at the moment.'

'That's a very nice dress you have on, dear,' said her mother. 'You ought to wear something like that more often.'

'My sentiments entirely,' he grinned, eyeing the revealing neckline and the way it hugged her curves.

Charley glared. It was as bad as the yellow one, worse even. She felt like a tart.

'Is it new, love?'

'Borrowed,' she snapped. 'It belongs to one of Braden's lovers.'

His thick brows lifted. 'Correction, Charley. Estefa is merely a friend.'

'A friend who leaves her clothes at your house? Humph! Some friend.'

'Charley!' Shock widened Isobel Blake's eyes. 'That's very rude.'

Charley eyed her mother and then Braden. 'I'm sorry.' But he knew she did not mean it, and he looked more amused than anything else.

'Don't worry about your daughter, Isobel. She and I understand each other perfectly. Ah, Juanita, this is Señora Blake. You have her room ready?'

'Sí, sí,' said the woman at once. 'You come this way.' Her skirts rustled as she ascended the wide marble staircase.

'I'll go and do my unpacking,' said Charley.

'And then we'll have a nightcap together.' Braden's voice arrested her flight.

She turned, her eyes cold. 'I don't think so. I think I might have an early night, too.'

'I want to talk to you, Charley.' His tone suggested that he was not going to take no for an answer.

'What about?'

'My research. I want you to start on it first thing in the morning, and as I shan't be here I——'

'If it's work, OK,' she said, and carried on up. She felt his eyes boring into her back and could not resist turning round when she got to the top.

'Don't keep me waiting long,' he warned tersely.

Charley hung away her clothes, changed into a pink cotton jumpsuit, assured herself that her mother was all right, and then made her way back downstairs.

She found Braden in his study. It was a big room with deep chairs as well as office furniture, and he stood with a drink in his hand, waiting for her. He frowned when he saw what she was wearing. 'Did you have to put that on?'

'It's comfortable,' she said.

'And unladylike,' he snarled. 'What will you have? Brandy? Scotch? Wine?'

'Brandy please.'

He poured a small measure into the bottom of a beautiful crystal glass and handed it to her. 'Sit down.'

She obeyed and took a sip of the gold liquid.

Lowering himself into the companion armchair, Braden stretched out his long legs and looked completely relaxed. 'How was Spencer this evening?'

'Asleep for most of the time,' she admitted. 'and very emotional when he saw my mother.'

Braden nodded. 'He said to me this morning that he needed her. I'm glad she's come because now there's no excuse for you to keep rushing away.'

'I like that,' she charged. 'I've been once.'

'But you would spend all day and every day at the hospital if I'd let you.'

'Of course I would. He's my father and I love him.'

'Naturally. But I have work I want doing, and soon.'

Charley eyed him keenly. 'Who would have done your indexing if I hadn't been available? Estefa?'

'If I hadn't met you, I'd have done it myself.' Braden's tone was suddenly sharp. 'Don't forget I gave up valuable working-time to search for your father.'

'I don't suppose you'll ever allow me to forget,' Charley retorted crisply. 'OK, so let's see what it is I've got to do.'

She made to get up, but Braden gestured her back down. 'There's plenty of time for that. Enjoy your brandy.'

Why had she got this feeling that talking work was only an excuse? Charley twisted the glass round and round and tried to ignore the tingling sensation that crept through her limbs.

'Is something bothering you?'

She had been looking absently down at the swirling liquid, now she saw that he was watching her give-away movements. 'I hate sitting doing nothing,' she prevaricated.

'You mean you hate sitting with me?' The sudden flare of his nostrils told her that the thought displeased him.

'You said you wanted to go through your notes.'

'I also asked you to join me for a nightcap.'

'You don't like drinking alone?'

'I don't mind, but when I have guests I like their company.'

'And anyone will do if Estefa's not available?'

His face darkened. 'What the hell have you got against Estefa? You've not even met her.'

'I don't need to,' said Charley quickly. 'The fact that she leaves her clothes here is evidence enough of the sort of relationship you enjoy.'

'And it bothers you, does, it, the thought of me having an affair with Estefa?' His eyes were narrowed and watchful, and Charley had to school her feelings carefully.

'You can have an affair with a different girl every month. It wouldn't worry me.'

'Then why this obsession? It's you who brings her name into the conversation.'

'Let's say I'm intrigued,' said Charley airily. 'Am I likely to meet her?'

'A woman's eternal curiosity,' he jeered. 'But, yes, I would say it's very likely. She's in Paris at the moment, though.'

'Where does she live when she's at home?'

'In Lima.'

Charley could not quell the unreasonable jealousy that rose in her throat like bile. There was only one reason why a woman would stay here when her own home was so close.

'Are there any more questions?' A sudden smile played on the corners of his mouth. He knew exactly what she was thinking.

'No.' She finished her brandy in one mouthful and almost choked as the fiery liquid burned its way down her throat.

'Then we may as well get on with the job we're here for.' He rose and crossed the room, and Charley followed, wishing she were not so sexually aware of him. It made things very difficult.

He pulled folder after folder out of his drawer, each full of scribbled notes and printed pages, of photographs and drawings, and of goodness knew what else. Charley's eyes widened.

'Yes, it looks a bit of a muddle, I must admit. There
are notes from years back here, some stuff I've used,
some I haven't. But it might come in. It needs careful
sorting and indexing so that I know exactly what I've
got.'

'It looks a lot of work,' said Charley, a faint frown
licking her brow. 'I shan't know where to begin.'

He nodded. 'I originally intended putting everything into my computer, but as you haven't that skill
index cards will do, cross-referencing them to the
notes and filing them in either alphabetical or
chronological order. I'll put it in the computer at a
later date. My recent findings are already in there.'

'You've not had it long, then?' Charley was
impressed, and she suddenly wished she knew how
to work this magic machinery. It was a skill everyone
in the business world needed these days, though she
had never envisaged finding it useful herself.

'No, and I'm still feeling my way around. Ramón's
a wizard at it. He's doing the graphics and all the
artwork, leaving me free to do the actual writing.'

It sounded very interesting, and Charley was
suddenly eager to begin. She peered at the closely
written pages. There were so many of them, all of
which had to be read before she could even begin to
index them. It would take her weeks. Her father
would be better long before all this work was
accomplished.

'These are the index cards,' Braden went on. 'I've
already given most of them headings. You may need
more. This, for instance——' He leaned across her and
picked up one of the sheets of paper, and Charley felt
sure it was no accident when his hand brushed her
breast.

She caught her breath and flinched away from him, and his mouth hardened. 'This would be filed under "Food". It's all pretty basic stuff. If you have any queries and I'm not here, ask Ramón.'

'When do you hope to begin the actual writing?'

'I've already started,' he admitted. 'But I have to keep stopping to dig out certain facts.'

Charley frowned her puzzlement. 'Surely, with your experience, it's all in your mind?'

Braden shrugged. 'Knowing what will interest an adult and what will interest a child are two different matters. I've never written a children's book before. It's going to be harder than I thought. Do you know much about children, Charley?'

'Not really,' she admitted.

'That's a pity. I thought you might be able to help me. Do you like children?'

His question surprised her. 'I suppose I do. Having no nephews or nieces, I've never had much to do with them.'

'Would you like children of your own?'

She gave a short laugh. 'What is this, an inquisition?'

'I was thinking how little I know about you. Do you intend to get married one day or are you too independent for that? Will your career as an explorer take precedence?'

There was a hint of mockery in his tone now which irritated Charley. 'Of course I'd like to get married. What woman wouldn't?'

'But there's no one special in your life at the moment?'

'That's right.'

'Have you ever been in love?'

'I think that's my business,' she said abruptly.

'Which suggests that you haven't,' he replied at once. 'And shall I tell you why? No man likes a girl who dresses and behaves like you do. Forget women's lib. Forget equality. Men still like their women to wear pretty clothes and do jobs that women are best equipped to do.'

In other words, he did not like her doing what she did. He did not like her dressing in this manner. In fact, he did not like her at all. An unutterable sadness filled Charley's heart. 'Have you quite finished?' she asked, and was surprised how steady her voice sounded. Inside she was trembling like a jellyfish.

'If I've made my point clear.'

'Oh, yes, you've made it clear. Very clear,' she answered bitterly. 'But if you think it will make any difference, you're mistaken. Surely, if a man loved me enough, he would accept me as I am?'

'Accept you, yes, but like it, maybe not. Isn't loving all about wanting to please one another?'

'Let's say,' said Charley angrily, 'that I've never been deeply enough in love with a man to want to change myself for him.' Which was a lie. If Braden loved her as she loved him, she would wear whatever pleased him most. She would take pleasure in dressing up for him. He was right in that respect. But there was no way she was going to try to impress a man whose opinion of her was nil. There was no point. All it would do was make her look a fool. 'This is a ridiculous conversation,' she snapped. 'I'm going to bed.'

She swung away, but Braden caught her arm and pulled her roughly towards him. 'Not yet, you're not. Ramón disturbed us earlier. Now there's no one to interrupt.'

But, even though her body cried out for his,

Charley knew she had to deny him. Letting Braden kiss her was insanity. She had been wrong in thinking she could store away memories and happily gloat over them at some future date. The pain in acquiring those memories was nothing short of torture.

'No, Braden.' Charley shrugged off his hand, and with her palms flat on his chest pushed with all her might, but she might as well have tried to demolish a brick wall.

'Stop fighting.' Braden took her wrists and, pinning her arms behind her, brought his hard body up against hers.

Charley's breath caught in her throat. Contact sensitised every nerve-end, making battle suddenly impossible. 'What's the matter, can't you wait for Estefa?' she demanded hoarsely. 'I'm sure she's far freer with her favours than I am.'

'Let's leave Estefa out of this,' he snarled.

'Why should I, when it's obvious she's very much a part of your life? But if it's not the thought of her that's turning you on, what is it? The fact that you're having to fight? Does that give you——'

'Charley!'

The tightening of his mouth should have warned her, but she went on, 'I imagine I'm a rarity, but even so it doesn't give you the right to——'

'Shut up, Charley.'

'The right to paw me whenever it takes your fancy,' she continued recklessly. 'If you're really all that hard up for sex then I imagine there are plenty of girls who'd be willing and——'

His mouth closed brutally on hers and a torrent of white-hot feelings rushed through her body. She had been right to try to keep him at bay. She felt in danger of melting in his arms, and struggling was futile. He held her in a vice-like grip, grinding her lips back against her teeth until she was forced to open her mouth.

Allowing him to get through to her was her weakness. She wanted these kisses. She wanted him as much as he wanted her, though for a very different reason. She had still not fathomed out what his was.

Slowly Charley's resistance drained, and when he realised she was no longer fighting Braden's mouth gentled. His arms slackened and it was sheer eroticism when he ran the tip of his tongue over her lips before feathering kisses along her jawline and down her throat.

Charley's head sank back as she gave an unconscious whimper of satisfaction. Why had she fought when every tiny part of her cried out for him, craved him, responded to him? *'Oh, Braden!'* Charley was not even aware that she had spoken. It was a cry from the heart, wrung out of her by the sheer intensity of her pleasure.

His mouth moved lower, each hindering button undone, until finally he slid the jumpsuit down over her shoulders. Charley was beyond protesting. She lifted her arms out of it, arching her body towards him, inviting him, biting her lower lip and not even feeling the pain of it as his mouth closed over the darkened tip of her breast.

Even baser emotions were aroused as his tongue and teeth tormented her, primitive feelings ignited. She needed support, her legs suddenly incapable of holding her weight. Groping behind her, Charley felt the edge of his desk and leaned against it. Now she ran her hands through the thickness of his hair, holding his head against her, her face contorted with the delicious pain of his lovemaking.

She wanted more, she felt an aching need, and when he lifted his head and straightened his back Charley thought for one horrified moment that he was going to move away. Quickly she pulled his face towards hers, and this time it was her tongue that traced the firm line of his mouth and probed the moistness inside. She let him see by every sensual movement and every tiny breath she drew that she was now ready for him.

'No, Charley.' He gently but firmly put her from him.

'But, Braden, I need you.' It was a plaintive cry and it would never have been dragged from her if he hadn't sent her half out of her mind.

'I'm doing myself no favours either,' he clipped.

Charley frowned. 'I don't understand.'

A muscle tightened in his jaw. 'Any fool can arouse a woman and have her begging him to make love. That's not what I want.'

'Then what do you want?' Her blue eyes were dark with anguish.

'What I want is—impossible.'

'What sort of an answer is that?' she asked him fiercely.

'The only one you're going to get. If you can't work it out, then I'm not going to do it for you. You'd best cover yourself up or you'll get cold.'

Charley was shivering already, but it was anger that made her limbs tremble. He had humiliated her. He had made her feel cheap. He had deliberately aroused her, and when she was on the verge of offering herself to him he had rejected her. God, she hated him. No, she didn't. She loved him still. Tears filled her eyes. It was a cruel emotion. And he was a cruel man. He had been cruel and merciless in the jungle and he was equally merciless now. *What he wanted was impossible.* What was that cryptic remark supposed to mean? She savagely stabbed her arms into her suit and buttoned it up. Braden was standing by the door and he held it open. She was dismissed. Walking across she looked him squarely in the eyes. 'Don't ever touch me again, Braden Quest.'

Charley thought she saw pain flicker in his eyes, but it was probably her imagination. Why should he be hurt? 'I'll do your indexing because I feel I owe you that, but from now on our relationship is strictly a business one.'

He nodded. 'If that's what you want.'

It wasn't what she wanted, damn him, but it was the only way she would ever get through these next weeks. If he dared to touch her she would be putty in his arms, and one humiliation was enough.

Once she reached her room Charley's control broke. Tears raced down her cheeks and dripped off her chin. She did nothing to stop them, merely falling to her knees and cradling her head in her arms on the edge of the bed. Silent sobs racked her. She refused to make a noise in case Braden heard and came to investigate. It would be the final degradation.

The next morning Braden had already left the house when Charley got up. She phoned the hospital and was told that her father had spent a comfortable night. 'I'm glad you're here, Mom,' she said over breakfast. 'I couldn't have done Braden's work otherwise. I'd have had to go and see Daddy.'

'I'll give him your love,' smiled Isobel. 'You'll be coming tonight, of course?'

'Try keeping me away.'

'I don't know how I'm ever going to repay Braden

for finding your father.'

'I shouldn't bother to try,' said Charley sharply. 'He's getting his payment out of me.'

Isobel Blake frowned. 'Are you in love with Braden?'

Charley looked abruptly at her mother, her heart hammering. 'Whatever makes you say that? I hate him. Isn't it obvious?'

'No, it's not,' replied the older woman firmly. 'I've never seen you like this. You're a changed girl when you mention his name, and last night the air positively crackled. And I'm not talking about tension or hostility, even though you were throwing verbal abuse at him.'

'You're wrong, Mom, there's nothing between me and Braden.'

Her mother smiled knowingly and shook her head. 'I think it's called body language these days, and you certainly give every impression of being attracted to Braden.'

Realising the futility of continuing to deny it, Charley lifted her shoulders in an expressive shrug. 'I never realised you were so astute, Mom. I thought I'd hidden my feelings pretty well.'

'Then you do love him?'

'Foolishly, yes.'

'And Braden?'

'Goodness knows what he feels. I wish with all my heart that I could get out of doing this work for him. It's going to crucify me staying here.'

'This Estefa you mentioned. Is he in love with her?'

Charley shrugged and took a savage bite of her croissant. 'He says not, but I don't believe him.'

'Has he ever, I mean, have you and he——'

'If you mean has he made a pass at me, then the

answer's yes. But it meant nothing to him,' she added quickly. 'I think he's frustrated because Estefa's not here. All I hope is that I'm gone before she gets back from Paris. I couldn't stand seeing them together.'

Her mother looked thoughtful, but said no more, and soon she had left with Carlos for the hospital. Charley made her way to Braden's study. She settled herself at his desk and began to read through the first folder of notes.

Braden's writing was difficult to decipher, but after a while she got used to it and was soon lost in the world of the Incas.

'It must be interesting.'

Charley clapped a hand to her mouth, suddenly shocked to see a grinning Ramón El Gordo standing over her. 'You frightened me half to death,' she accused him.

'Sorry, I did not mean it. How are you doing? Juanita tells me you have been in here hours. I think you ought to stop and join me for a cup of coffee.'

How attractive his accent was. She glanced at her watch, amazed to see how time had fled. 'Yes, please.'

He moved to the other end of the office and she noticed a coffee-pot on the low table. 'You brought that in with you?'

Ramón nodded. 'You were truly engrossed.'

'I love anything to do with the Incas. They've fascinated me all my life.'

'You are a remarkable girl.'

Braden doesn't think so. The words were on the tip of her tongue as she sat down in one of the deep chairs, but she held them back. 'I've always enjoyed exploring with my father.'

'He must be very proud of you.'

'He wanted a son, I guess that's why I'm as I am.'

'Yet you have not lost your femininity. Black or white?'

'White.' *And tell that to your friend.*

'You are very beautiful, Charley, as I am sure you must have been told many times. I think Braden and I are lucky to have you working with us.'

'I'm glad I can help out,' she said demurely.

He pushed her coffee-cup across the table. 'Help yourself to sugar. And a biscuit, perhaps? Juanita makes them herself. They are delicious.' He put a couple in his own saucer and sat down in the other chair. 'I am glad, Charley, that Braden has had to go out today. It will give you and me the opportunity to get to know one another.'

Charley felt a warning bell in her head. 'I don't think we ought to spend time talking,' she said. 'There's a lot to do and I've not even started.'

He brushed aside her protest. 'Braden will not expect you to make much headway today, I am sure. How long do you think your father will be in hospital?'

'A few weeks, I imagine,' answered Charley, nibbling a biscuit. She wished he would take his eyes off her. He was making her feel uncomfortable.

'Obviously I am sorry for him,' he smiled, 'but it is good news as far as I am concerned. One bad thing about working here is that there is a shortage of female company.'

'But you are married, are you not, Ramón?'

He shrugged, his dark eyes flashing. 'Braden told you? A pity. But just because a man is married it does not mean he cannot admire a woman still.'

'And I like to be flattered,' she agreed with a

disarming smile. 'But please make sure it goes no further than that. I am not into affairs with married men.'

'A brush-off, no less,' he said in mock dismay. 'But you cannot blame me, *señorita*. You are too, too charming.'

Charley was wearing a dress this morning, one of the few that she possessed, but it was nothing special. A button-through cotton with short sleeves and a tie belt, and she thought he was going over the top with his flattery. Maybe seeing her in the nude yesterday had done it?

'And you are a charmer yourself,' she smiled, drinking her coffee and standing up. 'Now I shall get back to work.'

As she moved past his chair he stood up, too, and caught her hand. 'I've not offended you, Charley?'

'Of course not.' Her smile was sincere.

He lifted her hand to his mouth. 'I would not wish to do that.'

At that moment the door opened and Braden walked into the room. He frowned harshly when he saw them standing close together. Charley tried to back away, but Ramón insisted on clinging to her hand.

'Braden,' he said, looking not in the least embarrassed, 'I did not expect you back so early.'

'Obviously not,' commented Braden harshly. 'Would you mind telling me what the hell is going on?'

CHAPTER NINE

RAMÓN EL GORDO'S teeth gleamed whitely against his dark skin as he smiled at Braden. 'It is simple, my good friend, I am merely appreciating a pretty woman.'

'Señorita Blake is here to work, not to be made love to,' snarled Braden.

'Charley has been working for many hours.' The man's brows rose disapprovingly. 'She was simply taking a well-earned break.'

Braden looked coldly at Charley. 'Is this so? Show me what you have done.'

'I haven't actually started indexing yet,' she began. 'I——'

'As I thought.' His chin jutted arrogantly. 'Maybe it's not such a good idea throwing you two together. I will find you another room in which to work, Charley.'

'That is not necessary,' said Ramón stiffly, his pride now offended. 'I will not bother her again. I did not realise that she was your private property.'

Braden's eyes narrowed. 'She is not mine in the way you are suggesting, but while Charley is under my roof I feel a certain sense of responsibility for her.'

'I think,' countered Charley sharply, 'that you are over-reacting. Ramón was merely being friendly.'

Braden turned his gaze on her. 'You're forgetting that I know him much better than you do. I like Ramón, do not get me wrong, and he is an excellent artist, but where the opposite sex is concerned he has a voracious appetite. Is that not so, Ramón?'

The other man pulled a wry face and shrugged. 'I cannot help it. It is in my blood.'

'And marrying Carmen made not the slightest bit of difference to him,' Braden told Charley. 'Fortunately he's never been found out. But one day he will not be so lucky, and then woe betide him. Carmen has one hell of a temper. I don't want you, Charley, to run the risk of being caught in the middle of such a confrontation. Now I suggest you get back to work.'

The rest of the day was uneventful and Ramón went home at about four. Isobel returned from the hospital in time for dinner and Charley went back with her for a couple of hours.

Her father looked no different, still a very tired and very frail old man, though she supposed it was too early yet to expect any change. 'Tell me what you've been doing today.' His smile was weary, though his interest genuine.

'Nothing much,' she shrugged. 'Mainly reading through Braden's notes. It's such interesting stuff, I get carried away. The time's fled.'

'He came to see me this morning.'

'He did?' Charley's eyes widened. 'I didn't know that.'

'He was passing by and called in.' Spencer looked thoughtful all of a sudden. 'Braden's just how I've always imagined a son of mine to be.'

Charley met her mother's eyes and Isobel lifted her brows but said nothing.

'The more I see him, the more I think it. I've always admired the guy, but his real personality never came across in his lectures. I'm so pleased that you and he have become friends.'

'Dad, I'm merely working for him,' insisted Charley gently. 'Once we're home I won't see him again.'

'Maybe,' said her father. 'He's in England often, he told me so. I imagine he'll call in to see us. I think we've made a friend for life.'

Charley's feelings were mixed. One half of her groaned because she knew a clean break was the only answer, the only way she would ever get him out of her system. But conversely she felt elated. Maybe he would grow to love her too, But she knew this was wishful thinking. If Braden had any feelings at all in her direction they would have surely developed during the time they had been thrust together. His only feelings were sexual, they went no deeper than that.

The next few days followed a similar pattern. Ramón took every opportunity to chat to her, and the innuendo was always there, but Charley kept him light-heartedly at arm's length. Braden was brisk and businesslike and she never saw him alone, but she often caught him eyeing her thoughtfully and she wished she knew what was in his mind.

The indexing progressed steadily and Charley loved the work. It would be a sad day when she eventually left. She would like to help Braden with the book. He had begun writing again and often came to the desk installed especially for her, bending over the index cards or leafing through the pages, setting her nerve-ends on fire by his closeness.

Then one day he told her that he had to go into Lima. 'I'm going to see my old friend Robert Kinsey at the archaeological and anthropological museum. I'd like you to come with me.'

They dropped her mother off at the hospital and

then Carlos drove them to the museum. While Braden talked to Robert, a likeable Englishman in his fifties with a jolly face and a paunch, she made her way slowly round the museum.

It was divided into various collections, all fascinating in their own right, macabre or otherwise, like the Paracas room with its examples of deformed heads, and skulls that had had part of the bone cut away to relieve pressure on the brain. More hair-raising still was the 'frozen' male mummy with fingernails still visible. The fixed sideways glance from his misshapen head was enough to send Charley hastening from the room.

There was an Inca room, too, with impressive models of the ruins at Machu Picchu and Tambo Colorado, but as she had already explored these sites they held no great interest.

When she found her way back to Robert's office it was time for lunch. 'I'd love to join you,' the older man said, in response to Braden's invitation, 'but unfortunately I can't get away. Next time, perhaps?'

'You must come up to the house,' insisted Braden. 'You're always promising, but I never see you.'

'Perhaps I will. As a matter of fact, I might come sooner than you think.' Robert smiled warmly at Charley, his eyes admiring. 'From what I hear, you're a very interesting young lady. I'd like to hear about some of your experiences.'

A muscle tightened in Braden's jaw. 'Yes, do that, Robert. I'll arrange a dinner party and your *wife* can come, too.'

'She'd love it,' he grinned, sublimely ignorant of the reason behind his friend's invitation. 'She's one of your greatest admirers.'

Outside Braden scowled and Charley did not see

why Robert's interest in her should provoke such a foul mood, nor why Braden was being so proprietorial. He had said it was because she was under his roof, but her mother was there, for heaven's sake. She didn't need his protection. Besides, she was perfectly capable of looking after herself. She wasn't in the habit of encouraging men—Ramón and Robert were being friendly to a stranger in their country, that was all.

'Where are we going for lunch?' she asked, trying to pretend that she had not noticed his attitude.

'We're going home,' he said bluntly.

'Oh, but I'd hoped to look around afterwards. I've never spent much time in Lima itself.'

'You're forgetting we have work to do.' His tone was crisp and brooked no argument. Charley gave a mental shrug. What had been the point in her coming?

Carlos arrived as if by magic with the car and they climbed inside. There was an uncomfortable silence until Braden said, 'You remember that guy who came out here and disappeared, the one you thought might have some connection with your father going missing?'

Charley nodded and frowned.

'According to Robert he's turned up in Ecuador. He had a fall and blanked out part of his memory. He has no idea how he got there. So all your worries about him and your father being killed by hostile Indians were completely unfounded.'

'I'm glad,' said Charley. 'I don't like to think the Indians would attack innocent men.'

'They wouldn't,' said Braden fiercely. 'But no one could blame them for making a mistake when for the last four and a half centuries Peru has attracted invaders intent on taking away its riches. I don't mind telling you, Charley, that I'm not proud of my ancestors.'

'Pizarro had a lot to answer for,' she agreed, glad he was taking his anger out on these early Spaniards instead of on her. She wondered whether he was putting as much feeling into his writing. She had seen none of it yet. 'What character are you portraying in your book?' she dared to ask. 'Pachacuti?'

'The Emperor?' His eyes widened 'Most definitely not. A mere tribesman. The children will be able to identify more readily with him. Of course, to cover the whole of the Inca empire I shall need to split the book into several parts, using a different character in each one.'

'I'd like to read what you've written,' she said hesitantly, half expecting a firm rebuff.

To her surprise he nodded.

They were out of the centre of Lima now with its banks and office blocks and shops, and were driving through the densely populated slum area where water taps and lavatories were frequently shared by several families. Charley hated this part. The total contrast of modern Miraflores, some seven or eight kilometres away, was welcome, and soon they were pulling up outside Braden's beautifully restored mansion.

There had been no further conversation between them, Braden settling into a brooding silence, Charley afraid to speak in case he snapped her head off. She refused to accept that a single remark by Robert Kinsey had done this to him. Something else must have triggered it off, nothing at all to do with her. She was being too sensitive, that was all.

But the moment they got indoors Braden's good humour was miraculously restored. And Charley's spirits dropped into her shoes.

A tall, dusky-skinned girl flung hrself at him. 'Braden, *querido,* where have you been?'

Estefa, thought Charley bitterly. Who else would greet him like this?

'I came early especially to see you, and there was no one here except Ramón and Juanita.' There was a petulant note to her well-modulated voice. 'I've missed you so much.'

The kiss that followed was too embarrassing for Charley to watch. They were devouring each other, or at least Estefa was devouring Braden, and he seemed in no hurry to put an end to the kiss.

When finally they pulled apart Braden looked towards Charley who was doing her best to fade into the background. 'Come and be introduced. I know you've been longing to meet Estefa.'

The swine, she thought, but the smile on her face gave away none of her feelings. Instead, it was the other girl who frowned. 'Braden, who is this?' And she clung even more possessively to his arm.

He smiled at her indulgently. 'This is Charley Blake. She and her mother are staying here.'

'Why?' the girl pouted, her eyes suddenly filled with suspicion. She had beautiful eyes, dark and almond-shaped, with finely plucked eyebrows. Her face was long with classically high cheekbones, her mouth wide, her lips full and sensual. There was no denying that she was very beautiful. Her glossy black hair was drawn tightly off her face and coiled into a chignon in her nape. She was elegance personified. Charley wondered whether she was a model.

'It's a long story,' he said, 'I'll tell you later.'

Estefa made no attempt to take Charley's outstretched hand, simply looking at her haughtily and with intense dislike. Charley dropped her arm to her side, feeling gauche and schoolgirlish. There was no comparison between her white cotton skirt and blouse and Estefa's silk designer dress in vibrant peacock blues and greens. It suited the dark girl to perfection.

'I've so much to tell you,' said Estefa, ignoring Charley and smiling into Braden's eyes.

'All in good time. At the moment I'm starving. Have you and Ramón eaten?'

Estefa shook her head. 'I couldn't eat a thing until I'd seen you.'

Her tone was husky and sensual, and Braden's answering smile suggested that he understood perfectly how she felt. 'Charley,' he said, with a brief glance in her direction, 'run along and tell Juanita there'll be four of us for lunch, there's a good girl.'

Charley's blue eyes flashed her anger and she felt like telling him to do it himself. But it was the excuse she needed to get away from the cloying atmosphere that suddenly surrounded her. She swung on her heel without a word and headed for the kitchen.

Juanita was surprised to hear they were back, but promised lunch in half an hour. Charley did not feel like eating now, only the fact that Braden might guess at the reason for her absence made her join them.

'Braden tells me that you enjoy crawling about in the jungle,' said Estefa with a delicate shudder, her sloe-shaped black eyes resting thoughtfully on Charley.

'Crawling isn't exactly the word I would use,' answered Charley evenly, 'though yes, I do like exploring.'

'As far as I'm concerned, it's a man's world,' the girl husked, glancing archly at Braden.

'Charley's a very liberated woman. She believes she can do as well as any man,' he informed her.

'And can she?' asked Estefa.

Braden looked at Charley across the table and slowly smiled. 'Almost.'

Charley grew warm inside, but the next second he had turned his attention back to Estefa and she could have willingly thrown her knife at him.

Ramón, at her side, sensed her outrage and whispered in her ear, 'Do not let him see your green eyes.'

She glanced at him in alarm. He knew?

'Yes, I have guessed your secret,' he murmured, his tone still too low for the others to hear. 'But do not worry, it is safe with me.'

'More cold meat, Charley?' Braden's hard voice interrupted them and it was evident by his set jaw that he was displeased. He probably thought Ramón had been whispering sweet nothings.

'No, thanks,' she answered coolly, meeting the steady glare of his eyes. 'But how about you, Ramón? I'm sure you could eat some more.' She picked up the plate and held it out for him to take what he wanted, conscious all the time of Braden watching them.

'Braden.' Estefa pawed his arm, reminding Charley of a spaniel trying to curry favour. 'Do you think I could have a teeny little bit more of that salad? It's so delicious. I've certainly missed Juanita's food.'

With one final glare at Charley and Ramón he turned his attention back to his beautiful friend. 'Of course, eat as much as you like.' He ran his eyes over her svelte figure. 'Have you lost weight while you've been away? You really should eat more, you know, it's——'

'I've been pining for you,' she said huskily. 'It's

the longest three months I've ever spent.'

Three months away from Estefa? thought Charley. So that was why he had shown an interest in her. It was too long for a man as virile as he to go without. At least it cleared one thing up in her mind. She knew now without a doubt that his interest in herself had only been transitory.

'If you'll excuse me,' she said faintly, 'I can't eat any more. I'll go and start work.'

Braden frowned. 'You've hardly eaten enough to feed a sparrow. Aren't you well?'

Her chin went up. 'Perfectly well, thank you.' Just sick about Estefa.

'I'll be with you soon,' said Ramón softly.

Braden's nostrils flared in the characteristic way Charley had noticed when he was angry. 'Me, too.'

Immediately Estefa pouted. 'But how about me? You can't neglect me, Braden, the day I come back. Why don't we go and lie by the pool and catch up on all the news? And when our lunch has gone down we can swim.'

'Estefa, you're forgetting how busy I am. I can't just drop everything.' His tone was gentle, his smile warm. 'But maybe I'll finish early.'

'Promise?'

He dropped a light kiss on her petulant lips. 'I promise.' And he ran his fingertips down the side of her face. 'Why do I always let you get your own way?'

'Because you love me,' she laughed lightly.

Charley pushed back her chair and left the room without saying another word. She felt choked and near to tears. Did he have to make it so obvious that he preferred Estefa? Couldn't he do his lovemaking in private?

She sat at her desk but could not concentrate on her work, staring blankly in front of her, wondering how she was going to get through the next few weeks.

Ramón joined her and touched his hand to her shoulder. 'Why do you not let Braden see how you feel?'

'How can I when it's so obvious it's Estefa he prefers?' she protested. 'But even if he didn't, he doesn't love me. I'm not his type.'

'Do not put yourself down, Charley,' he said firmly. 'You are a very attractive girl. You do not have to look like a model to win a man.'

'But it helps,' she said miserably.

'Nonsense. The Estefas of this world are the sort men take to bed. They marry girls like you.'

Her eyes widened. 'Are you saying that Braden isn't going to marry Estefa?'

'I very much doubt it. Estefa has other ideas, but Braden—no, I do not think so. In fact, I am sure of it. He has known her a long time, they are close friends, I cannot deny that, but it does not break his heart when they are apart.'

Charley began to feel better. 'How much time does she spend here?'

'As much as she can,' admitted Ramón. 'More time than she does at home with her parents, unfortunately, but they both have commitments which means that they do not really see all that much of each other.'

'What does Estefa do for a living? Is she a model?'

'She's a dancer, and a very good one, I believe,' he told her. 'The show in Paris had rave reviews and they are talking about a world tour.' He smiled wickedly. 'Which will leave you a clear field.'

Charley grimaced. 'By then I shall probably be back

home.'

He shrugged. 'Who knows what will happen? Personally, I think Braden is a fool if he lets you slip out of his hands. You seem so right for each other. Estefa has no interest at all in anthropology.' His lip curled derisively. 'Just the state of his bank balance.'

By the time Braden joined them they had settled down to work. Charley glanced at him as he came into the room and their eyes met. The familiar tingle of awareness washed over her and she was the first to look away. She could not take much more of this.

He sat down at his desk and was still for so long that Charley glanced across at him. He was watching her. 'What's wrong?' he asked.

She frowned. 'I don't know what you mean.'

'You normally eat like a horse.'

'Oh, that.' She lifted her shoulders indifferently. 'I'm not hungry.'

'But you were earlier, in Lima.'

'And what I ate filled me up. Really, Braden, do I have to suffer an inquisition every time I leave some of my food?'

'I'm worried about you.'

'Don't be, I'm fine,' she snapped.

'Just so long as there's nothing wrong.'

'There isn't.

Silence reigned and the next time she looked at him he was smiling to himself. Charley felt cold anger ride through her. No doubt he was thinking about Estefa. The black mood that had settled over him earlier had completely disappeared.

After an hour he stood up. 'It's no good, I can't concentrate. I'm going for that swim.' He halted in front of Charley's desk. 'How about joining us?'

'No, thanks,' she answered quietly.

'I'm giving you time off,' he frowned. 'Why don't you take advantage of it?'

'In that case,' she smiled 'I'll go and visit my father.'

They left the office together, and outside the door he said, 'Is it Estefa?'

'Is what Estefa, for heaven's sake?' she demanded.

'The reason for your odd behaviour.'

He was standing so close to her, Charley could feel the warmth of his body, and every one of her pulses screamed out its awareness. But her answer was cool. 'Your friend doesn't bother me. You're imagining things.'

'I don't think so,' he said softly, brushing the back of his fingers against her cheek. 'But we'll play it your way for now. Give your father my regards.' And he walked away, whistling.

His touch had seared her, and when Ramón came out of the office she was still standing there. He looked surprised. 'What are you doing?'

'Just going,' she answered quickly.

'Braden?'

Charley nodded.

'Remember you are better than Estefa—and that is from an expert on women. Can I give you a lift?'

Her smile returned. 'Yes, please. I don't want to ask Carlos in case Braden needs him. Can you wait while I change? I won't be a minute.'

He grinned. 'Show me the woman who only takes a minute. But yes, I will wait.'

Charley would have liked a shower, but contented herself with a quick wash. She pulled on a yellow button-through dress, ran a brush through her hair and was downstairs in three minutes flat.

Ramón had brought his car to the front door and he

carefully handed her into it. As they pulled away,
Charley looked back and saw Braden standing
watching them. All he wore was his black swimming-
trunks, and even as she looked Estefa appeared at his
side in one of her minuscule bikinis. She tugged at
his arm and he turned and smiled down at her and
they disappeared into the house.

Charley clenched her fists. No matter what Ramón
said, it was easy to see which one of them Braden
preferred.

Her parents were surprised and pleased to see her.
'Braden has a visitor so he's given me some time off,'
she announced.

They accepted her explanation and Spencer told
them about the treatment he was receiving. He had
nothing but praise for the nursing staff. Isobel
agreed. 'I must admit I was worried,' she said, 'when
I knew they were keeping him here. But not any
longer.'

'How about if we go and eat somewhere in the
city?' asked Charley, when dinner time approached.
'Then we can come straight back.'

Her mother nodded. 'That would be lovely.
Braden's not expecting you?'

'I don't think so.' He probably wouldn't even
notice she was missing.

'You say Braden has a visitor?' asked her mother
when they were settled in one of Lima's first-class
restaurants.

'That's right—Estefa.'

'The girl whose clothes you borrowed?'

Charley nodded.

'What's she like?' ventured Isobel softly.

'Exactly as I imagined. Like a fashion-plate. I hate
her.'

'And Braden, what is his relationship with this girl?'

Charley shrugged. 'What do you expect? She was all over him. I couldn't take any more.'

Isobel Blake grimaced. 'It might not be what it seems.'

'Maybe not, but that doesn't help me. I shall be glad when we go home, Mom. Why does the first man I fall in love with have to be someone who doesn't love me?'

'It's part of life, love. You're either meant for each other or you aren't. Only time will tell.'

When they finally got back to Braden's house he met them in the hall. 'Hello, Isobel, how is Spencer this evening?' His voice sounded normal but his brow was dark with anger and Charley wondered what was wrong. Had he argued with Estefa? There was certainly no sign of the other girl.

'A slight improvement, I think, though it's hard to tell.'

'It will be a long job, I'm afraid. He'd gone so far.'

Isobel nodded. 'If it wasn't for you he wouldn't be here at all. I'll be eternally grateful to you, Braden. Will you excuse me if I go straight to bed? I don't know what it is about hospitals, but they always make me tired.'

'I'm ready for bed, too,' said Charley.

'I'd like a word with you.' Braden's tone hardened slightly.

Charley frowned. They seemed to have played this scene before. Was his anger directed at her? And if so, why? She mentally shrugged. 'Goodnight, then, Mom. I'll see you in the morning.'

'Goodnight, love. God bless. Goodnight, Braden.'

He took Charley's arm and propelled her through

into his sitting-room. There was a chair drawn up to the window, from where the drive was clearly visible. He must have been sitting there waiting for her to come home, jumping up the second he saw the taxi.

'What the hell's going on?' he demanded, closing the door with his heel and spinning her round to face him.

'What do you mean?' Charley was genuinely puzzled.

'You and Ramón.'

'Me and Ramón?' she echoed incredulously. 'He took me to the hospital, that's all.'

'Is it?' he barked.

'You think we've spent the whole evening together?' she frowned.

'What else am I supposed to think?'

'You've only got to ask my mother,' Charley cried. 'But is it really any of your business? I'm a free agent, Braden. Because you've given me a roof over my head it doesn't mean you can dictate what I do or what I don't do in my spare time.'

'I warned you about getting involved with him,' he rasped. 'Carmen phoned. To say she's angry is putting it mildly. You were seen with Ramón.'

'In his car, on the way to the hospital, yes, but that's all. Who saw me, anyway? No one here knows me.'

'I don't know who saw you, but that hardly matters. She phoned here to check whether he was working.'

'And you told her he'd gone out with me?'

'Do I look stupid?' he demanded. 'But it won't be long before she finds out.'

Charley shook her head, unable to take it all in. 'I wasn't with Ramón.'

'Not all the time, maybe.'

'Not any of the time. This is ridiculous, Braden. I've done nothing, for pity's sake. If Ramón picked up some other girl after he dropped me off, then that's his problem.'

'Are you sure it wasn't you?'

'Yes, Braden, very sure,' she answered impatiently. 'May I go now?'

He studied her for a long, hard minute, then his shoulders relaxed. 'I'm sorry.'

She lifted her brows. 'Please don't apologise, it's out of character. I'm quite used to your accusations.'

'I only know what I saw.'

'Yes, and I know what I saw. Estefa ushering you back into the house. You obviously weren't concerned enough about me going off with Ramón to come after me. Where is she, by the way? Waiting in your nice comfy bed? You'd better hurry. I don't imagine she likes being kept waiting.'

'Estefa's gone home.'

Charley's eyes widened. 'Poor you,' she mocked drily.

Braden's mouth twisted in amusement. 'If I didn't know better, I'd say you were jealous.'

'But you do know better,' she cried, cursing her mistake, resolving never to let him see how hurt she was again. 'I really have no interest in your affairs. I merely thought you could do a little better than her. She doesn't look the type to settle down and get married.'

'Who's saying I want to settle down and get married?'

Charley shrugged. 'It's what most people want.'

'Let's just say I'm very choosy. Marriage is a life-time commitment so far as I'm concerned. I have no intention of being dragged through the divorce courts after only a few years. I would have to be very, very sure about the woman I married, and she would need to feel the same about me.'

She nodded. 'I admire your sentiments and I wish you luck.'

'Don't you wish those same things for yourself?' His eyes were intent upon hers, making Charley melt inside, wishing it were her he could feel these sentiments about.

'Doesn't everyone?' she countered. 'But it doesn't always work out.' There were probably thousands of girls suffering from unrequited love, and the only solution was to make a clean break. It was what she would advise anyone. But in this instance it was impossible. She was caught in a trap, and until her father recovered there would be no release.

Braden's brows drew together in a frown. 'Are you speaking from experience?'

Charley lifted her shoulders. 'I might be. Can I go to bed?'

'I've not finished with you yet.'

She closed her eyes in a weary gesture and then opened them again smartly when she felt his mouth on hers. Much as she wanted and needed him, however, she could not stomach the thought of him coming to her straight after Estefa. Using every atom of her strength, she pushed him away and ran from the room.

CHAPTER TEN

'*AMA sua, ama llula, ama quella*. What do you think of that for a title?' Braden looked at Charley with his head tilted to one side.

'I'd tell you, if I knew what it meant.'

'Shame on you, Charley. It's the Incas' three commandments. Don't lie, don't steal, don't be lazy.'

'In which case, it would be a very good title,' she said, 'except that I don't think any kid would pick up a book with a name like that. Why don't you use it as a frontispiece?'

'Good idea. Why didn't I think of that?'

'Because I have more brains than you.'

A week had passed since the day Charley scorned Braden's kiss, and they now existed on an uneasy truce. Light-hearted bantering on the surface, but smouldering hostility beneath.

Estefa was always about, making sure that Charley knew Braden was her private property. And the more Charley saw them together, the deeper grew her hurt. Braden never actually took Estefa out, but that did not matter. They were here, together, either swimming or locked in conversation in one of the rooms. Maybe his bedroom. Charley did not know. She just knew they disappeared for hours at a time.

Braden worked mornings and kept his afternoon free for the other girl. If it hadn't been for Ramón, Charley would have gone out of her mind. He flirted outrageously, but there was nothing serious in his intentions. Now that he knew she loved Braden he made no demands on her, merely trying to keep her in a cheerful frame of mind, bolstering her ego, and refusing to let her brood.

'Braden is a fool if he cannot see what is right under his nose,' he said to her one afternoon. She was standing at his desk looking at the graphics on the screen in front of him. They were reproduced from an Inca drinking-vessel, and the result was both ancient and modern at the same time. The children would love it.

'Maybe I'm the fool,' she said. 'I should never have let myself fall in love with him.'

'Love is not an emotion you can control. It happens when you least expect it.'

'That's true,' she admitted. 'Braden was the last person I thought I'd ever love. But it's killing me, Ramón, seeing him with Estefa. I wish I had the courage to leave.'

'Booking into a hotel would cost money and solve nothing.'

'You're right; besides, we owe him such a lot. Sorting out his papers is the very least I can do. I wish I knew how to use the computer, I could put them in there for him.'

He grinned. 'Then you really would make yourself indispensable.'

'Couldn't you show me, Ramón?' she asked with sudden excitement. 'I'd love that, I really would.'

'And how about my artwork? Braden would not be happy if I neglected that. I am afraid there is not time, Charley. It is a pity, I would be more than happy to be your teacher.'

He put his arm about her waist and pulled her to him. 'Even if it was only for the excuse of having you close.'

She bent her head and laughingly kissed him. 'You're incorrigible.' Then she pulled out of his embrace. But as she turned away Charley was confronted by a mountain of a woman with flashing black eyes and a murderous expression. A torrent of abusive Spanish was hurled in their direction.

Ramón stood up and ineffectively tried to calm the angry woman. 'This is my wife,' he said apologetically to Charley. 'Unfortunately, she thinks we are having an affair. Carmen, no!'

The woman had begun to pick up things and throw them, flinging them at him with all her strength. Books and pens, a box of paperclips and a staple gun, a pair of scissors, a box of floppy discs containing precious information, each one accompanied by harsh invective.

Ramón tried to control her, but in her anger Carmen possessed superhuman strength, and in the end all they could do was stand and watch, shielding their bodies from the more dangerous objects.

Carmen had just picked up a chair and was about to crash it over Ramón's shoulders when Braden walked in. He took one look at the scene and barked something in fluent Spanish. Carmen looked sulky but put down the chair. Her tongue was not silenced, though, and as she poured out a stream of complaint her dark eyes continually shot from Charley to Ramón. It was not difficult to guess what she was saying.

Braden spoke to her calmly and at length, until gradually some of the woman's tension eased. She would have been beautiful if she did not carry so much weight, decided Charley. She probably had been when Ramón had married her. But it was easy now to see why he was attracted to younger, slimmer girls. It was a pity.

'Ramón, I think you had better take Carmen home,' said Braden after a while.

The older man's eyes were distressed. 'I must explain. There is nothing between Charley and me. What Carmen saw was——'

Braden cut him short. 'Do not give me your excuses,' he snapped. 'Carmen is the one you should be talking to. Take her. And I think it might be best if you do not come back here until Charley has gone home to England.'

'But——'

'No, Ramón. I mean it. I saw this coming a long time ago. I warned Charley what would happen.'

Ramón looked coldly at Braden. 'If you opened your eyes properly you would see an entirely different picture. I shall not be coming back. You can find someone else to do your artwork.' And to Charley, 'I am sorry. And maybe I have been wrong and you are right. You should leave also. Whatever you decide, may I wish you every happiness.'

'Thanks, Ramón,' Charley said quietly.

When they had gone a heavy silence settled over them. Charley stood and surveyed the devastated room. Braden stood and looked at her. Before either of them could speak Estefa appeared in the doorway. 'I thought I heard something. Goodness me, what's happened?'

'Nothing that you need concern your pretty head about,' said Braden, smiling at last. 'Charley's just going to clear up the mess, aren't you, Charley?'

Her chin jerked. 'I don't see why I should'

'Every reason, since it's all your fault.'

She glared, then, hunching her shoulders, turned her back on him, refusing to retaliate. Besides he

wouldn't believe her if she denied an affair with
Ramón. He had made up his mind about that long
ago.

When the door closed behind them Charley
dropped to her knees and cried. But not for long.
Tears soon gave way to anger, anger against Braden
for his unfairness, his biased outlook, his inability to
see that she was eating her heart out for him. Why
was life so unfair?

The door opened again and, expecting Braden,
Charley was surprised to see Juanita. 'The *señor*, he
send me to help.' Her eyes widened in astonishment
as she took in the chaos. 'You have a row? You and
Braden? You throw things at each other?'

Charley could not help smiling. 'No. Didn't Braden
tell you what happened?'

'He say an accident.'

Some accident, thought Charley. She nodded.
'Sort of. I don't know where to begin.'

'You leave it to me. You go to your room.'

'No.' Charley was adamant now. 'We'll do it
together.'

She began to pick up the invaluable discs, keeping
her fingers crossed that they hadn't been damaged.
Most of them were filled with Ramón's graphics, and
if he wasn't coming back it would be impossible to
replace them.

It took a good half-hour to set the room to rights,
and by then Charley knew it was pointless trying to
do any more work. She went upstairs and took a
shower, and when she returned to her bedroom
Braden was waiting.

She pulled the towel more tightly around her and
eyed him aggressively. The last thing she wanted at
this moment was a confrontation with Braden. 'What

do you want?'

'Something Ramón said is puzzling me.' He walked over to the window and looked out, then he turned and leaned against the sill. 'What did he mean—if I opened my eyes properly I would see an entirely different picture?'

Charley shrugged. 'It's not for me to say.'

'What is it I am supposed to be looking at?'

'I can't tell you,' she said, wishing Ramón hadn't spoken those words.

'You discussed leaving here?'

'That's right.'

'Why?'

She closed her eyes. 'Because I'm not happy.'

His hands on her forearms made her lids snap open. 'Why aren't you happy here?' he demanded. 'Is it concern for your father? You want to be nearer to him? Is it because you don't like doing my work? Or perhaps you would prefer more freedom to be with Ramón. Is that it? Is it he I should be keeping my eye on? I did believe you the other day when you said there was nothing in it, but now I realise I was a fool. Carmen told me she saw you kissing him.'

'A friendly peck, nothing more. He's old enough to be my father, Braden.'

His nostrils flared. 'Precisely, but I believe some girls do prefer older men.'

'Thirty years older? I don't think so. You have a disgusting mind. On the other hand, I don't see why it should bother you if I did have an affair with Ramón.'

His grip on her tightened, and there was a frightening fierceness to his silver-grey eyes.

'I'm nothing to you, am I?' she demanded. 'You have Estefa. I wish you'd jolly well marry her and

be done with it and then at least I'd——' Charley
broke off as she realised she had said too much.

'You'd what?'

'Nothing,' she murmured, fighting back sudden
tears. 'Let me go, damn you. Let me go.' She
struggled free and glared at him from across the
room.

'You *are* jealous of Estefa, aren't you?' he asked
with a faint smile.

Charley turned away from him. 'Of course not.'
Yet even to her own ears she sounded unconvincing.

'Why don't you tell me the truth?' His tone was
low now and persuasive.

The truth! He could threaten to cut out her tongue
and she would never admit her love for him. How
could she? It would be far too humiliating. Suddenly
she wondered whether he had guessed. For what
other reason would he ask whether she was jealous
of Estefa?

'The truth, Charley.'

He had come up behind her and when she spun
round he caught her again and pulled her to him. Her
cheeks were burning. 'What truth?' she cried, stalling
for time. 'A moment ago you accused me of being
interested in Ramón, now you're asking me about
Estefa. I really don't see that your friends have
anything at all to do with me.'

'OK,' he said, 'let's take them one at a time. First of
all, Ramón. What are your feelings for him?'

Nothing like the ones that were racing through her
at this moment. Sparring with Braden seemed to
intensify her emotions. She wanted him to kiss her.
She wanted him to forget everyone else and concentrate solely on her.

'Well, Charley, I'm waiting.'

She dropped her head back and looked at him. 'I like Ramón, he's fun, he makes me feel good, but as for anything else, it doesn't exist. I'm not interested in him sexually.'

'But he is interested in you?'

'He was, until I made it clear I didn't want that sort of relationship. After that he didn't bother.'

Braden's eyes narrowed. 'That doesn't somehow sound like Ramón. His affairs are notorious.'

'He respected my wishes, strange as it may seem to you.'

'In that case, I may have done him an injustice.'

'That is for you and him to sort out.'

He nodded slowly, but his hold on her did not lessen. They were welded from stomach to knee and Charley was a mass of sensation.

'And now, Estefa. Tell me what you feel about her?'

'The truth?'

'Yes.'

'I think you're wasting your time,' she said boldly. 'You have no common interests. She's very sexy, I admit, but that's about all. Is that what you like? Is that what you're interested in?'

'Charley.' He touched a finger to her lip and smiled. 'We're not talking about my feelings for Estefa, but yours. Remember? A little thing called jealousy.'

'OK,' she flared, his faint mockery getting through to her where anger hadn't. 'I am jealous. I can't think what you see in her. She's empty-headed and I hate her.'

His eyebrows rose. 'May I be permitted to ask what promotes these harsh feelings?'

'Isn't it obvious?' she asked.

'Not to me.'

'We spent a lot of time together, Braden. I think I got

to know you pretty well. And in a strange sort of way I suppose I—care for you.' She swallowed hard. 'And that's why I don't like to see you making an idiot of yourself over some girl who's not worth it.'

He pulled a surprised face. 'I didn't realise I had such a staunch supporter. What sort of girl do you think I ought to choose? Someone like yourself, perhaps?'

Oh, if only he would. Again Charley swallowed. 'I don't know.'

'We have a lot in common, that's one thing in your favour.'

She nodded miserably and wished too late that she had held her tongue.

'And you're not overtly sexy, though that doesn't mean to say it's not there. I remember several occasions when I thought you looked exceedingly sexy.'

'We're not discussing me,' she said tightly, trying to ignore the rush of sensation that was threatening her sanity.

'Maybe you're not, but I am. I'm interested in finding out why this sudden concern over my affairs.'

'It's not sudden.' she said. 'I've never liked Estefa.'

'Would it please you to know that she's leaving for Italy tomorrow?'

Charley's heart lurched. It was the best news he could have given her. But she was afraid to show too much enthusiasm. She nodded demurely. 'Though I imagine *you're* disappointed?'

'I'm used to it,' he shrugged. 'She's never home for long.'

'But you make the most of it when she is?'

'Would I be human if I didn't?'

'I suppose not.' Men had a much stronger sex urge than women, and if it was offered to them on a plate they took it. 'So tonight will be your last one with her?'

To her surprise he shook his head. 'We've already said our goodbyes. She's gone home now to be with her parents. I thought maybe you and I could spend the evening together.'

Yes, yes, cried Charley's heart, but her mind saw red. For the second time she shrugged free of him. 'You have a nerve,' she hissed through her teeth. 'I'd never play second fiddle to Estefa, or anyone, for that matter. And if you think I'd give up precious visiting-time to be with you, then you're gravely mistaken.'

'I didn't intend you to miss seeing your father,' he said gently. 'I'll come with you. And then afterwards we can go out for a meal. We still have a lot to talk about.'

To her disgust, Charley found herself agreeing. Oh, God, why was she so weak? And she chose the prettiest dress in her wardrobe for the occasion, a coral pink with a full, swirling skirt. She had bought it for a party once and she had no idea why her mother had packed it. Not that it came anywhere near to the creations Estefa wore, but it was feminine, which was what Braden liked—*and why the hell did she want to impress him?*

Even her mother's brows rose when she came home that evening and saw Charley in the dress, and when she heard that they were going out for a meal she was delighted. 'How did this happen?'

Charley shrugged, her expression wry. 'Estefa's gone, she's off to Italy tomorrow, so Braden asked me out, and somehow I found myself agreeing. Don't get any wrong ideas, though. I'm second best so far as he's concerned. It will probably be a disaster.'

'Not unless you make it one.'

'It's not been an easy day,' sighed Charley. 'I've been

accused of having an affair with Ramón, and Ramón's walked out on Braden.' She went on to explain what had happened, and Isobel pulled a sympathetic face.

'Never mind, love. Things have a habit of sorting themselves out.'

Spencer was visibly pleased to see Braden. 'I was telling these two the other day that if I'd had a son I'd have wanted him to be like you.'

Embarrassed colour flooded Charley's cheeks, and her mother raised disapproving eyebrows. But oblivious of their reaction Spencer went on, 'I set my heart on having a son. I wanted him to follow in my footsteps. I wanted him to be as enthusiastic about the Incas as I am.'

'I don't think you can be disappointed in Charley,' said Braden quietly.

'Oh, no, don't get me wrong. She's the best daughter a man could wish for.'

'She's quite a girl,' agreed Braden, smiling gently at her, 'and I for one am glad she's not a boy.'

Charley felt every nerve-end quiver as she met his gaze. There was something new in his expression, a kind of softening towards her, but she knew it was only because Estefa had gone. It would be madness to respond.

After a few more minutes' conversation, Braden said, 'Would you mind very much, Spencer, if I whisked your daughter away? We're having dinner in the city.'

'Wonderful,' smiled Spencer, looking at Charley fondly. 'You must tell me all about it tomorrow.'

'I will, Daddy, I will,' she said, pressing a kiss to his brow. Her father was beginning to improve. His skin had lost that frightening waxen quality, and although he was still painfully thin he no longer looked like a living corpse.

'I hope you like Chinese food,' said Braden when they were outside, 'because I've booked a table at El Dorado.'

'I love it,' admitted Charley, and as the restaurant was within walking distance Braden told Carlos to stay and wait for Mrs Blake.

El Dorado was situated on the top floor of a skyscraper block with panoramic views across the city. Charley wished it was daylight, but even so the neon lights provided a breaktaking display. 'It's beautiful,' she said, her eyes shining. 'I never realised this was here.'

'There's a lot you don't know about Lima,' he said. 'I find it a most fascinating city.'

Probably because Estefa lived here, thought Charley. 'Do you intend to live here permanently?'

'Oh, no,' he frowned. 'I shall keep my house, of course, but England will always be my home. I only live here when I'm actually working on a project that needs constant research.'

'It's a pity about Ramón,' she said quietly.

His mouth firmed. 'Ramón is a fool to himself.'

'I've never been involved with him.'

Braden nodded. 'So you keep telling me.'

'How will you finish your book without his help?'

He shrugged. 'I suppose I'll have to find someone else. I'm no good at drawing.'

'I wonder if I could help,' she mused. 'I used to be quite good at art at school.' Even as she spoke the words, Charley knew she was an idiot.

His brows rose. 'It would mean staying on, perhaps even after your father returns home.'

Charley swallowed hard and nodded. 'Yes, I realise that. But I feel guilty. It's my fault Ramón walked out on you.' And she was talking a whole load of nonsense.

Wasn't the truth that she wanted to stay with him in the hope that now Estefa had gone he might fall in love with her? They had never really had a chance since they had come back to Lima.

'You surprise me, Charley, but yes, I'll accept your offer, provided you're good enough, of course. We'll see what you can do tomorrow.'

'I can't work the computer,' she admitted ruefully.

'They don't have to be computer pictures. I just thought the kids might like them.'

'I could always learn, though.'

'You're very anxious to please all of a sudden.' His brows arched questioningly. Charley blushed. 'And I like you in that dress. Do I flatter myself that for once you've dressed to please me?'

But that was too much for her to admit. 'Why should I do that? I simply thought the occasion demanded it.'

They nibbled their way slowly through the wide variety of courses placed in front of them, talking about the Incas and his writing and her father, but Charley was not concentrating. Braden's nearness was suffocating. She was breathing him in and mentally touching him and wishing and hoping that what he felt for Estefa was nothing more than physical.

'Charley, you're not listening to one word I say.'

'I'm sorry.' She had been looking at him and yet not looking at him. She had been studying the way his eyes creased at the corners when he smiled, the muscle that worked in his jaw when he was really intent over something, the scar that added to his attraction. The times she had longed to touch it with her fingertips, to trace its length, to smother it with kisses. She wanted to hold him, to feel him against her. And she wanted him to experience these same powerful emotions. She wanted to be a part of him.

'I was saying that it's ironic your father wishing he had a son, when mine always wanted a daughter. My mother died when I was twelve, and he wanted someone to remind him of her.'

'Don't we always want what we can't have?'

His grey eyes narrowed. 'There is something that you want?'

I want you, she said, but the words were not spoken aloud. She lifted her shoulders. 'I'm speaking generally.'

Still his eyes did not leave her face, and she moved uncomfortably.

'I've never heard you mention your father before,' she said to lighten the atmosphere.

'We don't see much of each other these days, I'm afraid, though I try to phone him regularly.'

'He lives in England?'

'In the New Forest, a beautiful part of the country.'

'By himself?'

Braden smiled. 'No, he's remarried, to a girl nearly thirty years his junior. So, you see, it's not so incredible.'

'I didn't fancy Ramón,' she said.

'I'm glad.'

'But I'm not denying that he didn't make me feel better.'

He frowned. 'Better?'

'I was lonely,' she returned quickly. 'You had Estefa, my mother was at the hospital all day, I had no one.'

'How would you have felt if neither Estefa nor Ramón had been present?' If you'd only had me for company?'

Ecstatically happy. Charley looked down at her plate. 'I don't know. Sometimes I hate you, sometimes I—like you.'

He paused, then said, 'For one moment I thought you were going to say you loved me.'

She glanced at him quickly to see if he was making fun of her, but his expression was perfectly serious.

'Hate and love are the same animal, you know.'

Charley swallowed hard. 'Are they?'

He nodded.

Her heartbeats quickened painfully and she could not seem to take her eyes away from his. There was silence for several seconds before he spoke again.

'So what is it, Charley? Do you love me?'

Oh, God, how could he ask her such a thing? How could he humiliate her in this manner? She closed her eyes, but the next moment he had gripped her hand across the table and she was forced to look at him again. 'Do you, Charley?'

'Why do you ask?' she whispered painfully.

'Because it's important to me.'

'Important?'

'That's right. I want to know. And I want the truth.'

The lump in her throat got bigger. 'I—I——' Tears filled her eyes.

He enclosed her hand in both of his, and his touch now was excruciatingly gentle. 'Yes?' he prompted softly.

'I love you.' It wasn't even a whisper. She painfully mouthed the confession.

'Let's get out of here,' he grated, signalling to a waiter for the bill. He took a wad of notes from his wallet and threw them on the table. Then her hand was caught once again in his and he hastened her from the room.

'I don't think you have any idea,' he said, as they waited for the lift, 'how much I've wanted to hear you say those words.'

'So that you could make a fool of me?' she whispered in agony.

'Hell, no! Oh, Charley, *Charley*.'

The lift came and they got inside, and the moment the doors closed he pulled her into his arms. She discovered he was trembling. His mouth hungrily closed over hers, and for the very first time Charley gave herself freely to him.

The kiss went on and on, and the lift got to the bottom. When the doors opened there were other people waiting to get in. Charley felt as though she were walking on air as he guided her outside.

'I love you too, Charley,' he said, hailing a passing taxi.

It was all too much for Charley to take in. 'But Estefa?' she demurred.

'Estefa is a friend, no more. I had an affair with her once, but that's been over a long time ago.' He helped her inside.

'I don't think Estefa wants it to finish.'

He smiled. 'She's a very affectionate person. Mostly it doesn't mean a thing. But I must confess I used her to try to make you jealous.'

Charley shook her head in bewilderment. 'How long have you loved me, then?'

'I was attracted to you right from the beginning. You were one hell of a female.'

She frowned. 'But you said all those hurtful things to me.'

'You were the antithesis of what I've always thought a woman should be. I fought against natural instinct.'

'And you treated me so hatefully in the jungle.'

'I always kept my eye on you, don't you ever think differently. But boy, do you have spirit. I admire you, Charley. You're the gutsiest lady I've ever met. Even when I tested you on that cliff path you wouldn't give in.'

'I have my pride,' she admitted. 'And how I've fought against loving you!'

'I wish I'd known sooner. It's been hard, denying myself. You responded so beautifully whenever I took the initiative, but I wanted more than that. I wanted you to make the first move. I wanted to know how *you* felt.'

'And I thought you were using me because there was no other girl available.'

'Charley.' He took her face between his hands. 'I've never done that to a girl in my life. I have complete self-control over my body. Except when I'm with you,' he added hoarsely, kissing her again. 'I remember the first time you really got through to me.'

She frowned. 'When was that?'

'The time you couldn't sleep and I got into your sleeping-bag.'

'And I thought I'd had a dream?' she asked suspiciously. 'It was a dream—in part, anyway. We were dressed up in evening clothes calmly hacking our way through the jungle. Then we found this quiet grassy spot and lay down and——'

'Explored each other's bodies?' he finished for her. 'I didn't realise until the next morning that you were actually asleep. I thought you were feigning it.'

'If I'd been awake, I'd have fought like a tiger,' she threatened.

He laughed. 'You did that often enough. I hope you never change, Charley. I like my fiercely independent woman.'

'You want me always to wear the trousers?' she grinned.

He cuffed her playfully. 'Only when we're in the jungle and as I intend to start a family straight away, I can't see you doing much of that.'

Charley's eyes widened. 'A family out of wedlock? Shame on you, Braden.'

'Charley Blake, you're going to be married to me before you know it,' he said sternly.

'Aren't you going to get down on your knees and ask?'

'Certainly not, I'm telling you. Haven't I always made the decisions for the two of us?'

'Yes, sir,' she replied smartly. The taxi was drawing up outside his mansion. 'Let's not go in yet,' she went on impetuously, 'let's go and tell my parents while they're together.'

But Braden shook his head. 'I haven't waited all this time to get you to myself to share you with anyone for the next couple of hours at least. But I'll tell you one thing we'll do. We'll have the wedding ceremony in the hospital. Your father will love that.'

'He'll get his son, after all,' she said as they walked into the house with their arms around each other's waists.

'Do you think he was throwing out a broad hint?' frowned Braden as the thought occurred to him.

'I don't think so, he's not that devious. Unless of course,' she went on slowly, 'my mother told him how I felt.'

'You mother knew you loved me?'

Charley nodded. 'I guess I wore my heart on my sleeve.'

'Did Ramón know?'

'Yes, he saw it too.'

'So I'm the only one who was blind to your feelings?' She nodded. 'But I didn't know how you felt, either.'

'I was pretty rotten to you—is it any wonder? God, when I think of the way I treated you sometimes . . .

How can you ever forgive me?'

'I think it might take me a very long time,' she said with a grin. 'You'll need to give me an awful lot of loving before I do.'

'In that case, dear future Mrs Quest, I'd better start now.' He pushed open the front door and swept her into his arms. They were half-way up the stairs before she struggled to free herself.

'If it's all right with you, Mr Quest, I'd rather wait until we're married. I'm a very old-fashioned girl.'

'Old-fashioned girls don't wear trousers,' he muttered. 'Only modern misses. And modern misses think nothing of going to bed with their prospective husbands.'

'My mother would be shocked.'

'You strike a hard bargain, Charley Blake. Have you any idea what's going on inside me at this moment?'

'Much the same as inside me, I imagine,' she smiled; 'But I think it's worth waiting for, Braden.'

He groaned and held her tightly. 'You're right, of course. But I'm warning you, I shall set things in motion first thing in the morning and the wedding will take place as soon as is humanly possible—like tomorrow afternoon,' he added with a grin.

'I don't care how soon it is,' she replied. 'I just want it to be right. Not very much has gone right for us so far. Perhaps this will be the beginning.'

He nodded gravely. 'Charley, I give you my solemn pledge now to do everything in my power to make you happy, for evermore.'

Charley felt tears sliding down her cheeks.

'Now what's wrong?' he asked, gently taking her face and wiping the tears away with his thumbs.

'Oh, Braden, you don't know much about girls, do you? I'm already happy, can't you see that? So very, very happy.' And the tears would not stop.

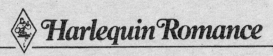

Coming Next Month

#3007   BLUEPRINT FOR LOVE Amanda Clark
Shannon West knows that renovating an old house means
uncovering its hidden strengths. When she meets Griff Marek,
an embittered architect—and former sports celebrity—she
learns that love can do the same thing.

#3008   HEART OF MARBLE Helena Dawson
Cressida knows it's risky taking a job sight unseen, but Sir Piers
Aylward's offer to help him open Clarewood Priory to the
public is too good to miss. Then she discovers that he wants
nothing to do with the planning—or with her.

#3009   TENDER OFFER Peggy Nicholson
Did Clay McCann really think he could cut a path through
Manhattan, seize her father's corporation—and her—without a
fight? Apparently he did! And Rikki wondered what had
happened to the Clay she'd idolized in her teens.

#3010   NO PLACE LIKE HOME Leigh Michaels
Just when Kaye's dreams are within reach—she's engaged to a
kind, gentle man who's wealthy enough to offer real security—
happy-go-lucky Brendan McKenna shows up, insisting that *he's*
the only man who can really bring her dreams to life....

#3011   TO STAY FOREVER Jessica Steele
Kendra travels to Greece without hesitation to answer her
cousin Faye's call for help. And Eugene, Faye's husband, seems
grateful. Not so his associate, Damon Niarkos, the most hateful
man Kendra's ever met. What right does he have to interfere?

#3012   RISE OF AN EAGLE Margaret Way
Morgan's grandfather Edward Hartland had always encouraged
the enmity between her and Tyson—yet in his will he divided
the Hartland empire between them. Enraged, Morgan tries to
convince Ty that he's a usurper in her home!

Available in October wherever paperback books are sold, or
through Harlequin Reader Service:

In the U.S.
901 Fuhrmann Blvd.
P.O. Box 1397
Buffalo, N.Y. 14240-1397

In Canada
P.O. Box 603
Fort Erie, Ontario
L2A 5X3

COMING IN OCTOBER

SWEET PROMISE

Erica made two serious mistakes in Mexico. One was taking
Rafael de la Torres for a gigolo, the other was assuming
that the scandal of marrying him would get her father's
attention. Her father wasn't interested, and Erica ran
home to Texas the next day, keeping her marriage a secret.
She knew she'd have to find Rafael someday to get a
divorce, but she didn't expect to run into him at a party—
and she was amazed to discover that her ''gigolo'' was the
head of a powerful family, and deeply in love with her....

Watch for this bestselling Janet Dailey favorite, coming in
October from Harlequin.

COMING SOON...

Indulge a Little
Give a Lot

An irresistible opportunity to pamper
yourself with free* gifts and help a
great cause, Big Brothers/Big Sisters
Programs and Services.

*With proofs-of-purchase plus postage and handling.

Watch for it in October!

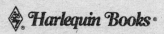

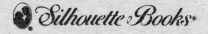